More Novels by G. Emslie.

Le Congo

San Mateo

Hit Man

Hesitate...Your Gone

The Mossad Man

Malaya

Dead or your Money back

Priest Killer

San Mateo

San Mateo

San Mateo is a story based on the adventures of a young Scottish backpacker, who accidentally got involved in the drug trade in California and eventually became the biggest drug dealer in Los Angeles. It is his journey, from an innocent hippy to a millionaire drug supplier and his inner struggle with good and evil.

San Matteo County, California.

CHAPTER 1

1965. Mid-June and the beach was a scorcher in California.

As I lay on the beach, my mind drifted back to my childhood.

I was an abandoned baby brought up in a brethren's compound, in the wilds of northeast Scotland.

It was rumoured that I was a child of one Lucy Walker. a young brethren widow who had an affair with a married guy in the late forties when an unmarried pregnant woman was frowned upon.

Being adopted by an elderly childless brethren couple, who by a strange occurrence was an uncle and aunt of the said, Lucy Walker! Being raised in the brethren community meant no TV, no newspapers, and no radio.

Education wasn't an important issue, learning the bible was more of an item. Nobody went on to high school or university. We were a closed society, where all our needs were taken care of, it was the only life we knew. The evil of the 'outside' world was drilled into us, so it was more 'risk-free' to stay in the brethren—within the 'cult.' Anyone that left and ventured into the world was so unprepared for real life that they begged for forgiveness and returned to the brethren, to be reminded of their mistake at every opportunity.

We were told that the devil travelled through the wires and that all newspapers contain lies and misinformation. We were only allowed to read the good book. At that age, I did not know anything else. On Sunday, we were up early to go to the chapel. The elder who gave the sermon was an old guy called Skinner,

a wiry, mean-faced individual, who would serve up a diet of hellfire, preaching that we were all sinners, destined to fall into the fires of hell.

In the chapel, the men sat on hard wooden pews on one side and the women on the other. Fraternising with the opposite sex on a Sunday would draw looks of disapproval!

5

The women never cut their hair but wore a hairband, a long dress down to the ankles and no make-up. The men wore a black suit with a white shirt and boots.

Skinner had a daughter, Alice, she was fifteen and a rebel with a dislike of her bullying father, and would tell me stories of saving her mother from his wrath.

After the sermon, we would meet up for a kiss and a cuddle behind one of the outhouses. One Sunday, Alice produced a bottle of beer! I was shocked and said,

'Alice, we will go to hell.' She giggled, we felt so naughty!

The school was a half-mile walk, along a mud road to a one-room wood and tin hut, with one teacher Mr. Down, who would at least once a day fly into a frenzy, throwing books at us and shouting obscenities, then just as suddenly he would sit down and light up his pipe, as nothing had happened. Years later I learned he suffered from shell shock in the last war!

Another shock to my system came one Saturday evening. Alice and I were at Reverend Skinner's house. It was dark and we were in an alcove snogging and drinking beer when a taxi pulled up outside the house. Skinner and another elder got out; the taxi drove off as Skinner staggered to the garden gate, fumbled with the latch and fell over onto the wet paved path. The other elder bent down to pick him up and fell on top of Skinner. Was I seeing things?

They were both drunk! Alice giggled. I was shocked, then Alice said 'My father is a drunkard.'

The next day was Sunday. In the chapel I stared in amazement at Skinner as he delivered a sermon, with bulging eyes and a red face he waved a bible above his bald head, telling the eager listeners

that we were all going to hell for our sins.

I looked across the pews at Alice, and we both grinned. Maybe we weren't all going to hell after all.

As I grew older, I wondered about the 'outside' world.

Growing older in that enclosed environment, I became rebellious, questioning everything. The elders would chastise me, making me sit in a cold empty room and giving me a bible with marked pages. I had just turned eighteen when I decided to get out of this environment.

CHAPTER 2

One night I packed my things, including my bible and left. I hitchhiked down to London, sleeping in barns and thumbing lifts. It was all a different experience but exciting! Wandering the streets, I saw a sign in a pub window. Help wanted!

I worked at that pub cleaning up, collecting glasses, and throwing the drunks out. My bedroom was in a storeroom, full of beer barrels sitting on either side of my camp bed. My roommate was a mouse who shared my leftover sandwiches.

That was when I first met Shirley. She was a forty-something bar fly, who had once been an attractive woman, The lines on her face told me that life had given her a raw deal; abusive men and the death of her daughter from a drug overdose had made her lose hope. Her only comfort was in a glass, and the company of fellow alcoholics, each one with a tale to tell of their downfall.

She was easy to talk to and I enjoyed her company. We would both laugh when she told me about the nutcases she had dated. One evening she asked where I lived, and when I told her in the storeroom with a mouse, she laughed saying,

'George, I have a spare room at my flat and could use the company.'

She gave me her address and then left!

At closing time, I collected my things from the bar and took a taxi to Shirley's flat. She made me some food, opened two cans of beer, and sat down for a chat. She smiled and said, 'It's good to have a guy around..' She took me upstairs and showed me the tiny attic room with a window that had a cracked pane. To me it was the grand hotel, it was a while since I slept in a proper bed. I put my things away and got into bed. I was awakened by Shirley getting into bed with me. By the light of the outside street lamp shining through the tiny window, I saw she was naked—I froze.

'Shirley,' I stuttered, 'But I've never!' Shirley kissed me and with a grin said, ' A virgin?' She smiled; 'I've got my work cut out here.'

Over the next few weeks, with Shirley's wide experience, I completed my sex education. She showed me what I had been missing. With my earnings from the bar, I dressed in sneakers, jeans and a bomber jacket. The black Brethren gear was binned!

Looking at the poster in the recruiting window. Join the army! I liked the idea of belonging somewhere. Stepping inside I spoke with the guy, who said that he would sign me up if I passed the medical. I told Shirley that I wanted to join the army, and she looked at me and smiled. 'George, you're such an innocent, but I think this will introduce you to the outside world.'

I joined up and was sent to a barracks in the south of England. Three meals a day and a lot of physical exercises. Just what I wanted. I joined the boxing team and got a few bloody noses, but I learned fast. I also joined a judo class, rising to a brown belt! I loved all the training and turned out to be a natural at judo, my confidence soared. I was in the army for two years, and left with the rank of sergeant, then journeyed back to London looking for some adventure.. The nervous Brethren boy had grown up!

I worked as a barman come bouncer, living in an upstairs attic room, basic but cosy! Throwing a drunk out of the bar one night when I saw a girl crying at the doorway, 'What's wrong Luv?' She told me that two guys had snatched her bag with her money and keys. Between sobs, she pointed to the other side of the street, where two teenagers were standing under a streetlight, searching through her bag.

I crossed over and spoke to them in a firm tone!

'Give the girl her bag back guys,' the tall one stepped up to me and snarled.

'Or what?'

Punching him on his jaw he dropped to the pavement. Grabbing the bag from the other guy as he ran off. She insisted on buying me a drink and over a beer she told me her life story, how she was thrown out of college for smoking dope, and how she threw her boyfriend out for cheating with her friend. The list of mishaps was endless, and that's how I met Carla.

One-week later Carla moved into my humble abode. She fussed about the room, taking the bedding to the launderette, picking up socks and pants off the floor and cleaning places that had not seen daylight for decades. Carla enjoyed a joint now and then, so I spoke to the local supplier to get some good stuff. She would light up, strip naked and do the ironing puffing on a joint—a nice sight!

I was getting restless, wanting to see more of the world. One evening out of the blue, Carla said, 'Let's backpack through Europe.' So, I packed in the bar job and we both set off to Paddington station.

We saw the Eiffel Tower. Took a boat trip down the Seine. Sat with tourists at the Cathedral in Cologne and drank wine with the locals in the arty cafes.

I had a few run-ins with guys at the student hostels, usually drunks. I had an arm-wrestling challenge with a little skinny guy in a bar in Cologne. Carla remarked, 'You can beat that cocky wimp.'

The bet was for a beer. He had a crowd of supporters cheering him on. As I struggled to force his arm to the tabletop he never stopped grinning. I had a feeling he'd done this before. He beat me easily to the cheers of his mates.

'Best of three?' I ventured. He beat me every time. The little shit was a professional. I got him a beer, then he did something that I hated. He patted my head as you would a child and grinned.

Better luck next time! he said. As I punched him, he fell backwards into the crowd. Then his mates attacked me like a pack of wolves, giving me a beating. Carla got a few punches from the women in the bar. The wife of the bar owner took pity on us, took us through to the bathroom and cleaned us up. Carla had a black eye. I had a bust nose and a swollen eye. We looked at each other and laughed. Carla grinned through a swollen lip, 'Never arm wrestle a wimpy-looking guy again.' We enjoyed travelling around Europe but we always wanted to see sunny California.

CHAPTER 3

Arriving in sunny San Mateo County, California. on Student visas. We picked grapes, washed dishes, walked dogs, anything that gave us enough bucks for a hamburger and a couple of beers. Staying at the farm where we were grape picking.

Living in a long timber shed, with about twenty other hippies and their girlfriends, kids and dogs. We had a metal bed, an old wooden wardrobe with, "I love Pam," carved into the door, and a hessian curtain for privacy.

In the evenings we lit a fire and sat around drinking beer and smoking hash. Some guy had a guitar, so we had sing-alongs and serious, 'sort the world's problems with a hippy college professor who had lost his job through drugs but had deep intelligent conversations with the older guys.

We would spend two or three days picking grapes and some days at the beach swimming and sunbathing.

Carla woke me with a beer and a sandwich.

'Come on let's cool off.' Holding hands, we jumped into the cold water of the Pacific. Life felt good with no stress.

Now and then the cops would come to the compound looking for the hash, and generally let us know to get our paperwork together, —but never checking anything. Two cops ran the show. Sam, a big heavy, middle-aged guy, who would take off his cowboy hat and wipe his bald head every few minutes and Hendry, a short black guy with two front teeth missing, giving him a lisp. I asked Hendry,

'How come you guys never check our paperwork?' he smiled, 'When the picking season is over, that's when we check your papers,' he laughed, 'Then we throw you bums out of the state and some guys out of the country.' Back at the farm and sitting around the fire. Carla said, 'George, the season is nearly over, I was thinking of going home to London and back to university, I miss my family.' This came as a shock as she had said this was paradise.

'OK Carla, we will stay till the season is over, then go back to London'—I Lied!

I didn't smoke hash myself, but everyone I knew did!

One night I went to a bar in the local town and got chatting with a black guy who asked if I wanted any hash. Shaking my head,

'No thanks.' He shook my hand and politely said.

'My name is Papa. Why don't you make yourself a few bucks by selling the hash at the farm?' I nodded and wondered how he knew I was a grape picker on a farm. Was it my scruffy hippy look?

'OK, anything to make a few dollars.' After we finished our drinks, he took me out to his car which was parked in the shadows at the back of the bar and gave me a small parcel from the boot saying,

'It is all in small rolls, you can charge three bucks a roll and you can always find me here on a Saturday evening.' During the following week, I sold all the hash for one hundred bucks.

At the bar the following Saturday, I met Papa, gave him the money and he gave me thirty dollars back—This was more than I made picking grapes! I asked Papa, 'How do you know that I wouldn't run off with the cash?' He grinned,

'I trust you, man. Do you want to sell some more hash?' I nodded, We stepped into the darkness of the car park and went to his car parked at the back of the bar. He looked around and then opened the boot. I glanced in and saw four big rug sacks. Opening one he handed me three small parcels. I stuffed them in my shopping bag and went back to the farm!

Word had gotten out that I was the man for selling cheap hash. The stuff was going like hotcakes. Carla and I were spending less time picking grapes and more time at the beach where she was permanently stoned with free hash.

One evening I returned to the farm and saw a big black Cadillac sitting outside the shed. As I came to it, a huge black guy wearing a yellow tracksuit and three rows of gold chains around his tattooed neck stepped out. 'Hi, man! I hear you're the guy selling the cheap hash?'

He put his hand on my shoulder and shook his head, 'You're on my patch. Sorry man, but you either find another marketplace,' he grinned showing a mouth full of gold teeth, 'Or you could wind up in a ditch on the freeway.' I put my hand on his arm and did my favourite judo throw. He crashed to the hard ground, bruised and dazed. His young friend got out of the car and came towards me with a knife in his hand, I sidestepped and punched him on the jaw, and he dropped to the ground—out cold!

Bending over the dazed guy I growled,

'You give me any hassle,' I put my face closer to his, 'I'll be around with my guys, for a visit.'

I helped them both into the Cadillac and waved them goodbye. I was shaking, I had heard of bodies being found in ditches with bullet holes in the head.

That night I lay awake, listening to every sound. I decided if I was to carry on selling hash, I needed protection—A gun!

The next day I got a visit from the cop Sam and his sidekick Hendry. I was sitting outside the shed with Carla, who was smoking a joint and telling me how much she loved life in the "camp," when they pulled up and got out. Sam took his cowboy hat off and wiped his sweating head. Hendry lit up a cigarette. Sam uttered,

'I hear you are selling hash?' He went on, 'I don't care if these guys and gals smoke horse shit, as long as it doesn't cause me any trouble! The season will soon be over, and you guys will be gone.' As they got back into the car, Sam buzzed the window down and said,

'I am kind of partial to Cuban cigars.' He winked and drove off.

I went into town with Carla. I had a little money to spend which was a nice feeling. buying Carla, a hippie dress and a huge hat with a ribbon and a bow.

I found a gun shop and picked out a small revolver a .22 for fifty dollars the owner said, 'I need ID before I can sell you the gun,' I said, 'I've left my ID at home, I'll come back tomorrow.'
Outside the shop, Carla wore a puzzled face, and asked,

'What ID?'

We started to walk away from the shop when a young teenage assistant from the gun shop walked up to us and whispered,

'Have you got a hundred bucks?'

He handed me the gun wrapped up in a bag, grabbed the cash and hurried back to the shop.

The next stop was the cigar shop. I had to keep sweet with Sam the cop. A box of Cuban cigars had a ticket showing twenty-five bucks. Showing my best shocked face I spluttered,

'How much!' The serving girl who had tattoos of birds on her neck and huge earrings was staring at her long-painted nails looking bored and without looking up said,

'Cuban cigars are hard to come by! Take it or leave it,'

'I'll take it, and two packs of cigarettes'—for Hendry.

We left the shop and started to walk away. I grabbed Carla and dived into a shop doorway. Carla said, 'What was that all about?' *I had just seen a big black Cadillac with four black guys cruising down the road. The driver wore a yellow tracksuit and rows of gold chains around his neck.*

I held my breath until the caddy drove past. I told Carla what had happened the other evening. She put her palms to her cheeks,

'O my god! These guys might kill us. Now I know why you bought a gun.'

We got a taxi back to the farm. Two guys and a couple were waiting to buy hash. The word had spread, these people were from the city. Over the next week, I sold all the hash with orders for more! That Saturday evening, I went to the bar to meet Papa. But after waiting an hour I asked the barman,

'Have you seen Papa?' He whispered,

'Papa was found by the side of the freeway last night, with a bullet in his head.' I ordered a whisky and downed it in one gulp, my eyes watered.

It was dark outside as I walked around the back of the bar, There was Papa's car, the door was unlocked, and the keys were on the sun visor. Opening the boot, I saw four zipped-up rug sacks. I got in and drove the car back to the farm. Carla helped me put the rug sacks into a small shed at the back of the living shed!

Taking Carla with me in Papa's car, we parked behind the bar. The two of us wiped the car interior clean, then went into the bar for a drink to recover from the drama.

The barman who served us mentioned,

'Another guy is asking around for Papa.' He pointed over to a smartly dressed older black guy, sitting in one of the booths. A huge mountain of a man, looking like an old-time wrestler was standing next to him. We took our drinks over to the booth;

'I hear you are asking about Papa?'

The guy looked up, 'Why don't you join me.' I told him about Papa's body being found on the freeway, he was quiet for a moment then said, 'Did Papa supply you with hash?' I told him it was just small amounts. He leaned over; 'Papa finished up dead because he did not pay his bills! Now I need to supply another source and you look like an honest guy; I think we could do business together.' He stood up, shook my hand and gave me his card, 'Let me know tomorrow.' He strode to the door, followed by the "Gorilla."

We finished our drinks and went back to the farm.

Sitting by the fire, Carla lit up a joint and said,

'What are you going to do?' Carla was puffing on the joint and I was in deep thought. She said, Let's do it till the season ends, then it's back to England,' I nodded, 'Sure, till the season ends.'

I rang the supplier; The name on the card was Mohammed. I heard a short laugh from the other end then he said,

'Please call me Moe, everyone does...even my mother.'

I told him I needed a couple of days to think about the deal! There was a pause then he grunted

'Don't be too long.'

Selling hash from the shed! I sold everywhere. I even got one of my customers to sell for me. I gave him a dozen bags, with the promise of more. One day I was sitting outside talking to a customer when a police car pulled up with Sam and Hendry. They didn't get out but called me over,

'Hi man, how's business? Got something for us?' he smiled, I nodded 'Wait there, Sam.' I went into the shed and came back with a box of "Expensive" Cuban cigars and a few packs of cigarettes for Hendry. Sam smiled, 'Thanks buddy, these will last me a couple of weeks,' he tapped his nose.

I had two thousand dollars from selling the hash, and still had two rug sacks left. I decided to go into the city to try and shift some more in the downtown area. I asked around which bars I could find dealers, there were a few. In one bar I went and got a drink. A little black guy sat on the next stool,

'Got any dope man?' I said. He pushed his drink away,

'It depends on what you're looking for.' As he reached over for his drink, I saw a police-issue gun and holster inside his jacket.

This guy was a cop! I muttered something about leaving my wallet in the car and got out of there quickly.

I now had enough cash to rent a decent apartment, so Carla and I rented a place overlooking the beach. One morning I left Carla making breakfast and went to a nearby store for some beer. Twenty minutes later I

14

returned and opened my apartment door, to see two black guys holding Carla in a chair, one had a knife at her throat. Slowly putting the beer down and looking at the guy holding the knife, I quietly said 'Take it, easy guys.' 'The tall guy, wearing a cap that said—*Capitano*---and gold-rimmed dark glasses, spat back,

'You take it, easy limey, where is the stack of hash?'

The one holding Carla was out of his mind and mumbling.

'Yeah, where's the stash.'

The tall guy stepped up close to me, I stepped to his side and punched him, and he dropped to the floor. The other guy lurched at me with the knife out in front of him. He caught me on the arm before I knocked him out!.. Carla fainted at the sight of blood. I went to the kitchen and washed the wound,

luckily it was only a slight cut. Carla staggered into the kitchen.

'I thought they were going to kill us; how did they know where we were?'

I went through the room in time to see them both disappear through the front door. That was a scary moment. I took the gun from the bedroom drawer with a shaking hand and stuck it into my trousers. We were both frightened. I thought this was the brethren boy dealing with the devil. I remembered Skinner's words. The wages of sin is death, how right he was!

Over the next two weeks, I shifted the other rug sacks of hash, I now had nearly eleven thousand dollars. One day I said to Carla,

'Let's go to Los Angeles for a break. It is getting a little dangerous here.' She nodded and said,

'Good Idea, I was hoping you'd say that.'

We packed up the apartment and took off to Los Angeles. Carla was usually off her head with hash by this time.

The drug scene in Los Angeles was huge, if you were dealing in the hash the cops left you alone, and sometimes a bribe was needed! The cops were only after the guys who dealt in cocaine.

I got in touch with Moe, he supplied me with all the hash that I wanted. We agreed that I would sell the hash, and then paid Moe.

I said to Moe, 'Why do you supply the hash upfront?' Moe grinned; 'I trust you and besides,' he grinned as he opened his coat showing a huge forty-five pistol in his belt.

Building up a huge clientele of lawyers, doctors, cops, housewives and Bums. I always gave them the good stuff, never mixing the hash with other stuff. I even gave credit to trusted customers.

One time I had a visit from the local Mafia. Two young "Italian" looking guys in smart suits and white fedora hats met me in my local bar, which was my office. They asked who was my supplier. and that they could supply good hash and cocaine a little cheaper I said,

'I don't touch cocaine and thanks. But no thanks.' The two young mafia guys sat down across the table from me. The short one leaned across the table and pointed his finger in my face. In a real Hollywood gangster voice, he snarled, 'I don't think you know whom you are speaking to.' In one quick movement, I snapped his finger. He screamed. Then I punched him in the mouth. The screaming stopped as he slid onto the floor. The other guy seemed shocked and then went for his gun. I beat him to the draw. He froze with one hand still on his gun handle. Leaning over and taking the gun out of his hand, I smiled, 'If you and your friend ever come into this bar again, I won't break his finger, I'll break his greasy neck...Comprendo.'

Knowing the guy who owned the bar, and giving him one hundred dollars every week to let me deal there. I said,

'I guess I am in trouble now!' He laughed,

'These guys are not the Mafia; they are small-time protection guys. They try and shake down the smaller dealers, but be careful, you have humiliated them and word travels fast.'

I was a little paranoid for the next couple of weeks. Every Saturday I would take Carla to lunch at an upmarket restaurant, then shopping or dancing at a late-night club. We also moved into a high-rise apartment block with views over the city, I felt a lot safer there, with a doorman on duty twenty-four hours.

The gun that I took off the Mafia gun was a pearl-handled antique with a silencer fitted. I swapped that one for my little revolver. I just hoped that the "Antique" wasn't a wanted gun.

16

I decided to broaden my business, with six guys in different parts of the city dealing for me. I paid them well and never missed them. Some tried to short-change me, but all in all the business grew. I had bought a nice Ford sedan to make my pickups. One evening I had a call for help from one of my dealers.

When I arrived, he was standing on the corner of the street corner, his face was all bashed up, 'Boss! They took my money and beat me up!' I got him into the car and used a first aid box to clean him up. I asked, 'Who took the money?' He mumbled through a swollen mouth,

'It was two Italian guys, One short guy with a big hat beat me up when I told them I wasn't interested. They said that it would cost me fifty bucks to deal here and that they would come to collect on Friday at eight. The other guy told me that they were taking over this part of town and they would supply me with cheaper dope to sell for them from now on.'
Friday evening at eight came around.

I parked the Ford in the shadow of some trees. It was dark as I stepped back into the shadows. I didn't have long to wait before a black Cadillac passed me and parked by the corner. Waiting in the shadows to see who they were. A guy got out and took a piss against the car. It was the short guy with the big fedora hat.

Holding my gun, I tip-toed up to him and smacked his head with the gun. He dropped to the ground still pissing onto his expensive trousers. Opening the driver's door, I saw he was alone.

Dragging the short guy into the driver's seat and taking his gun as he was coming around, I noticed he had a bandaged finger! Slapping his face, he stared at me and cursed,

'If I don't get the pleasure of killing you myself, I am going to pay a hitman to kill you, I don't care what it costs. He smirked, then I am going to fuck your bitch! He was still cursing as I shot him in the head.

Wiping the car door handle and looking around. There was music playing from one of the apartments. I drove my car along the freeway and stopped on the bridge. Throwing the gun into the river I drove back to my apartment and Carla

I filled a glass of whisky and sat on the sofa. My hands were shaking, I had never killed anyone before. Carla came out of the bedroom. 'Are you all right? your shaking, I think you've got a cold coming on.' I downed the whisky in two gulps, my eyes watered as Carla put a blanket over my shoulders.

The next morning, I was glued to the early morning news TV. The reporter said there had been three homicides last night. One unidentified man has been found shot dead in his car,

we believe it to be a gang-related shooting...Now for the weather.

I finished breakfast with Carla. She put her hand on my brow,

'You look a lot better, maybe it wasn't a cold!'

As I entered my local bar to deal, the owner came over to my stool and said, 'You know what, remember that little Mafia guy you knocked out, he has been found dead, not surprising Yeah?' I nodded;

'He must have had a lot of enemies.' I asked,

'Have the cops any idea who shot him?' The barman leaned over and whispered, 'No, they will put this one down to a gangland hit and close the case. There are killings like this happening every week, and the cops haven't the manpower, or the enthusiasm to chase up every criminal who gets shot!'

I breathed a sigh of relief at that news. My hand stopped quivering.

Deciding to do some good in the community to make up for my sins, there was still some of the brethren boy in me. I was now making thousands of dollars every week and living in a luxury apartment. I had a nice car and had the lovely Carla looking after me. With thousands of dollars stuffed in a cupboard, what more did I need? Peace of mind and forgiveness from the ghost of Rev. Skinner. I decided it was time to do a good turn.

I drove downtown to one of the roughest areas in Los Angeles, parked my car down an alley and went and found a soup kitchen. I joined a small queue of down-and-outs, mostly women with kids and drug addicts. When it came to my turn, I was handed a bowl of soup and a piece of bread. A nun came over to speak to me,

'You don't look like you need help. What is it you are looking for?' I looked at her and said. 'Forgiveness!' She had a knowing smile when she said, 'Well, why don't you start by helping out with the food? I am too busy feeding the hungry to forgive anybody right now. She made me look foolish and selfish.

Dishing out bowls of soup to a never-ending queue of unfortunates. I spoke to a middle-aged guy who told me that he had run a big corporation and lived a high life but succumbed to cocaine to ease the stress and had become addicted. He bowed his head as he recounted. 'I lost everything, my job, the house and my wife who walked out taking my son.' He wiped away a tear with a stained sleeve. Muttering as he shuffled away, 'Now home is a park bench or shop doorway.' He told me that he was "Clean"—but his eyes told a different story.

Discarded plastic bowls and the odd needles lying everywhere, I took a walk through the alleys and derelict houses and saw people huddled in cardboard boxes; I came across a couple with a child sitting in the doorway of a wrecked house.

They drew back as I approached. I asked the guy,

'How are things bud.' They looked at each other and both laughed. 'We are only staying here till our west side mansion is being redecorated,' She said. I smiled and handed the guy a fifty-dollar bill, but his smile disappeared, as he growled,

'What do you want man?' I shook my head,

'I'll settle for a smile' and walked away.

Further along the street, there were two guys and a woman, sitting on the ground sharing a wine bottle, I stopped and asked,

'How are you guys doing.' One of the guys asked,

'What are you looking for man?' The woman staggered to her feet, smiled and said,

'I know what this guy is looking for,' she lifted her skirt revealing no underwear! I handed her a fifty-dollar note and walked away to the sound of laughter.

The bottle hit me on the back of my neck, dropping me to the rubbish-strewn road. In a daze, I felt the two guys searching my pockets. I weakly pushed one guy off. As I struggled to stand, the other guy kicked me in the ribs, grabbed me by the throat and started to choke me. I struggled to pull my gun from my belt and jam it into his guts. He let go and stepped back with a curse, staring at the gun.

I walked back to the soup kitchen. The nun was shaving an old man with a cut-throat razor. He was sitting on a wooden chair with one leg shorter than the other three. Looking up she grinned,

'Have you found salvation?'

I shook my head, and she smiled, 'Look, young man, I forgive you your sins, does that help?' I handed her fifty dollars, and said,

'Put this to good use,' she thanked me and said,

'Now why don't you go home, I have to finish shaving this guy, besides, you don't fit in here!'

I walked to my car and drove back to my apartment, I asked Carla, 'How can I get rid of my sins,' she smiled, saying,

'What if I give you a good kick in the bullocks? Would that help?' We both laughed. Putting my sins to one side for now! I would have to figure something else out later—much later.

Carla and I flew to Zurich. with fifty-five thousand dollars to hide, there was no more space in the cupboard! The bank manager was very helpful! I explained that I could not carry a bank book or any paperwork, and he smiled,

'That is a common question in this bank!' He took me into a side room with a table. I put the money on the table. Then as a young woman came in carrying a tin box, the manager took a square item from the box.

'Now write your signature twice at the top, and press the digits of five numbers that you will remember at the bottom—all done.'

We had booked into a luxury hotel overlooking the lake. I ordered room service of smoked salmon and a bottle of Johnnie's Walker black-label whisky and Champagne for Carla. I ate the salmon and drank half a bottle of the whisky. Carla whispered,

'I would rather have a joint?' Knowing from experience that a hotel doorman can get you anything your heart desires—at a price.

I went down to reception and spoke to the doorman; He nodded; 'How can I help you, sir?' He whispered, 'Would you like the company of a young lady?' I smiled,

'Thanks, but all I want is a couple of joints.' He nodded and said,

'Certainly sir, any particular brand? Congo black? Highly recommended.' Back in the room, Carla was puffing away and getting high while I was enjoying the Johnnie Walker.

I sent down for some beers. Minutes later the waiter knocked. Carla opened the door, naked as usual.

We spent the rest of the day in bed. Then showered and changed and went down to the lavish dining room. Over the soup course, I passed out with my head on the soup plate. Carla went to the bar and was chatted up by a would-be film producer, who told her that for a fee of a "Paltry" ten thousand dollars he could get her a part in his next film. Carla was in a teasing mood. She put on her shocked, *"Really, you would do that for little ole me?"* look and asked the guy to get a cocktail while she thought it over. She took a sip and nodded,

'Yes I would love to be in a film,' she gushed,

'Tell me all about it. But first, get me another drink.' Then asked the guy if he wanted a cheque or cash.

CHAPTER 4

Flying back to Los Angeles the next day I picked up my car at the airport and drove back to our apartment. That evening, I drove around to some of my contacts, picking up the money and giving out more bags of hash. A couple of my contacts told me that they had been hassled by a Mexican gang asking them to sell their hash and cocaine. I asked around and found out the address of the Mexican boss.

He lived in a big mansion in an upmarket area. When I got there, I saw he had metal gates at the bottom of his drive with a security camera. I pressed the talk box. A voice rasped,

'Hello, what do you want?' I said I wanted to talk about his guys hassling my dealers, he laughed, 'Come in my friend?' The gates opened and I drove up to the house. A skinny young Mexican guy wearing a huge sombrero came out of the house carrying a rifle and patted me down. In his rush, he missed the little Derringer tucked in my ankle holster.

He showed me into a huge dining room, with wood-panelled walls and a Hollywood-style crystal chandelier. At the ornate Italian-style dining table sat an old fat Mexican guy smoking the longest cigar I have ever seen. A cloud of smoke hung from the ceiling, making the room stink of tobacco. He waved me to sit, with fingers covered in various gold and diamond rings. 'How can I help?' I took a deep breath and said, 'Stop harassing my guys,' He blew smoke into the ceiling, then growled, 'Look gringo! I just want to do business with you, You have a good name on the street, and people trust you and your hash, but I can supply you with all the hash you want, at a price that will make you smile. Good Mexican hash.' He leaned over to shake my hand. I didn't move as I lowered my voice,

'I don't need a partner; I need you to stop harassing my guys.'

He stopped smiling and put the cigar into the ashtray.

'Listen Hombre! You do business with me, or you will disappear,' I glared at him, 'I told you. I don't need a partner...Hombre!'

He shouted out to the young guard with the rifle.

'Take this son of a bitch to the ranch and shoot him!' He picked up the cigar and stuck it in his mouth. I bent down to my ankle holster pulled out my revolver in one movement and shot the guard twice. The fat Mexican's cigar dropped out of his mouth, making a shower of sparks as it hit the table. Putting his hands in the air he said,

'Don't shoot me, I can give you money!' Nodding to the bedroom door. He stood up and I followed him into a small bedroom. Standing behind him as he opened a small safe. He glanced at me and then pulled a gun from the safe. He spun around as I shot him in the head. Dropping to the floor, still holding the gun, his eyes stared into space and blood pooled around his head.

I listened for a moment, but all was quiet. In the safe were over a hundred and fifty thousand dollars, a list of names with phone numbers and a note with a safety deposit number.

I found a shopping bag in the kitchen and stuffed the money and papers into it. As I walked through the dining room the guard was lying on the floor moaning. I said, 'Sorry hombre, but you should not keep such bad company.' Then shot him in the head.

I found the switch to open the security gates and left in my car. Back at the apartment, Carla helped me search through the list of banks with safety deposit facilities. Over ten! We decided to go through every one. Carla rang a taxi. As we waited in the reception area, I spoke to the doorman about finding the bank that had safety boxes! I showed him the top half of the safety box slip. He patted my shoulder and smiled,

'The bank you are looking for is the Bank of America on Main Street!' I thanked him and we took the taxi to the main street. In the manager's office, he studied the safety box slip, and then took us downstairs to the vault. Opened a steel door and then into a room with walls lined with boxes. He opened a cover and pulled out a tin box, put it on the table, and left saying, 'Ring the bell when you are finished.' I tapped the code on the slip of paper into the digits on the box.

There was a click and the lid sprung open. The box was jammed with taped-up bundles of money.

Carla and I spent the next half hour counting. There were one hundred thousand dollars in high denomination notes and four diamonds in a pouch. Putting everything into her bag I rang the bell.

As we were leaving the bank a security man stopped us and said,

'Will you step into the manager's office for a moment sir.' I whispered to Carla to slip out with the bag, but the security guy stepped in front of her, 'You too madame, please.'

He led us into a large plush office, the manager was standing by the window staring out at the traffic. Waiting until we had sat, he sat down and shuffled some papers and said,

'I remember the last gentleman who accessed that safety box. He was a large Mexican gentleman. 'He stared waiting for an answer—I blustered, 'Yes. Yes, my cousin! He wasn't able to come today so he gave me all the details.' I sucked in a breath. *Supposing he decided to ring and check with my "Cousin"*

The manager was quiet for a moment, then nodded,

'Yes, of course, he looked unwell when he was here' We all stood and the manager shook our hands and took us to the door, 'How is your cousin's cough?' I smiled and said, 'I think he is cured.'

Back at the apartment, we put the hundred thousand dollars into a travel bag and the diamonds into my pocket. At the airport, the customs guys were coming to the end of their shift, so we were waved through. I had learned that customs men were human, after a long shift of irate travellers asking the same questions, they were inclined to wave everybody through in the last hour.

CHAPTER 5

The flight took nearly twelve hours, giving us a chance to plan, have a drink, read glossy magazines and sleep. When we arrived in Zurich, we booked into the airport hotel. A shower and change, then a taxi the six miles to the city centre and the bank. The manager recognised us and we were greeted with open arms.

'Welcome. Another deposit perhaps?' We deposited the money and asked the manager where we would find a diamond trader.

He wrote down an address and called us a taxi. Twenty minutes later we stepped out of the taxi at the original old town, a grubby run-down area, that was shaded from the sun by the huge modern office blocks.

An Arab-looking guy came up to us and said,

'Can I help you, sir,' Before I could say anything Carla said,

'We are looking for a diamond trader shop?' I quickly said,

'Yes, we are interior designers, here to decorate his office.' He pointed to a cobbled street with old wooden houses.

Walking up the street, Carla gave a little scream and grabbed my arm as a rat scuttled across the cobbles and disappeared into a gap between a pair of brick houses.

We found the shop and went in. Behind a wooden counter was an elderly Jewish guy with a long grey beard and John Lennon glasses perched on the end of his nose, Looking us up and down he looked puzzled. and said, 'We are about to close, what do you want?

I took one of the diamonds out of my pocket and put it on the desk. His face changed to a smile as he put a small magnifying glass to his eye, then called out to another guy who came through a hessian curtain from the back room and inspected the stone. Speaking in Yiddish to the first guy. He then said,

'Sir, where did this diamond come from?' I smiled;

'It was left to me by my maiden aunt!' Carla looked puzzled.

'How much do you want?' asked the older guy. I tried to sound like I knew the value of the stone.

'I know how much it is worth! What is it worth to you?' The two men spoke to each other in Yiddish. Then the older one said, 'Twelve thousand dollars.' I choked. *I would have settled for Twelve hundred.* I put my hand to my cheek and said,

'What!' The guy paused then spat out,

'OK. ok, fifteen thousand dollars, but that is our best offer.'

We shook hands and fifteen thousand dollars was counted out and put into Carla's bag. Coffee came through from the back room.

The little orthodox Jew said, 'My name is Obi, and you are?'

'Santa.' Carla smiled as she drank her coffee. I slid my hand into my pocket and pulled out another Diamond. Obi's eyes lit up; he called the older guy back. They both inspected the stone, then Obi said with a sly smile, 'We will need a discount on this one!' Picking the diamond off the desk; I muttered, 'I think we will look for another buyer?' Obi panicked,

'Wait, I was joking.' Another fifteen thousand dollars duly arrived and was stuffed into Carla's bag.

We had thirty thousand dollars, and still had two stones left!

We went back to the hotel and sat at the bar to celebrate.

Carla went to the toilet as I ordered drinks. I hadn't noticed the guy standing next to me. Carla came back after five minutes. Sitting down she asked, 'Where is my bag?' I looked around in time to see a guy striding out the glass swing doors with her bag under his arm.

I bolted through the big doors of the hotel, just in time to see the thief get into a taxi. Jumping into the next taxi in line I shouted, 'Follow that taxi and don't lose him.' I handed the driver a fifty-dollar note through the glass partition. After following through winding dark streets to the rough end of town, we pulled up behind a taxi outside a grubby-looking bar.

Quickly getting out and following the guy, *still clutching the bag,* into a crowded bar, he was holding the bag to his chest as he drank. I was afraid that he would see me and bolt, So, I stood at the back of the bar, behind a couple of guys. I watched as the thief spoke on the phone for a minute, then spoke to the barman, who pointed to a toilet sign. Finishing his beer, he went through the door marked gents.

Now was my chance. I followed right behind him, but he quickly darted into a cubicle and locked the door. I stood opposite the door at the urinal pretending to take a leak.

Suddenly the door opened. I turned around and pushed him back into the cubicle, closing the door. Punching him as hard as I could, twice. He collapsed onto the toilet, bleeding from his mouth and nose. *Where was the bag?* I pushed him to the floor and lifted the toilet top. halleluiah! There was the bag stuffed down into the cistern. Someone was banging on the door, and a voice yelled,

'What's happening in there?' I heard someone shout,

'Get the police!' I opened the door and pushed my way out of the bar just as a cop car with a siren wailing and lights flashing came screeching around the corner.

Quickly marching along that dark cobbled street away from the bar, I found a taxi and went back to the hotel.

'That was a narrow squeak?' Carla said, and laughed. I was covered in blood, so we both got into the shower and Carla washed the blood off me. We put the bag with the money into the hotel safe and went for a stress-free drink. I was nervous because many people had seen me at the bar and that thief was a mess.

The crowd might have thought that I was the robber, and the cops would have my description.

The next day we went shopping, Carla's favourite pastime. I sat outside the changing room while Carla was trying something on.

A guy was staring at me from the other side of the store. Cripes! It was the barman from the bar where I beat up the thief.

Pulling the curtain aside and stepping in.
Carla was standing in her knickers holding a dress. `I spluttered out. 'Quickly, put it on!'

Explaining the situation while helping her get the dress on. We went to the pay desk and gave the salesgirl the stub and the money.

Through the shop window, I saw a police car pull up. In a panic, I shouted, 'Where is the back door?' The salesgirl pointed to the door at the end of a walkway. We hurried out and piled into a taxi. The next day we flew back to Los Angeles, with thirty thousand dollars in her bag and two diamonds still to get rid of.

It was back to business as usual. One evening there was a knock at our apartment door, Carla went to the door and shouted, 'The police want to talk to you.' I heard a cop say, 'Mind if we come in.' I sat them down at the table. While Carla made some coffee, one of the cops looked around the room and said, 'Nice place you've got,—what business did you say you were in sir?' I smiled, 'Entertainment! What is it you guys want?'

The taller cop took a mouthful of his coffee and then said,

'A Mexican businessman and a security guard were shot dead last week, and your car was seen in the same area' I gulped;

'I often take a drive in that area.' The tall cop nodded, writing in a small notebook. 'Do you own a gun, sir?'

'Yes, it's at my office!' The cop stopped writing, looked up and asked, 'What kind of a gun is it?' I swallowed hard, 'It's a forty-five,' the cops stood up saying, 'That's all for now sir, but we may need to examine your gun?' Trying to sound casual I said,

'Sure, no problem.'

That evening as soon as the cops had gone, I took Carla for a drive along the freeway, stopping at the bridge. I handed her my gun and said, throw the gun over the bridge. Putting the car window down, she threw the gun into the darkness. It hit the bridge with a clang and bounced back onto the pavement. We scrambled out of the car and looked for it in the dark.

A couple walking their dog appeared out of the dark asking,

'Have you lost something?' I said the first thing that came to mind, 'Yes, a tin box.' They both started looking and then Carla found the gun. I snatched it from her hand and quickly threw it into the pitch-black river. The girl said, 'You found it, but why did you throw it into the river?' I smiled in the darkness, 'It was my grandma's ashes. She loved this river!' The girl smiled, 'Ah, that's sweet!' The guy said,

'I am glad you found it, I could have put up a notice at my police station,' the girl nodded, 'He's a policeman.' We shook hands. My heart was racing so fast I was sure he could hear it.

We sat in the car for a few minutes, till my heartbeat went back to normal! The next day, I spoke to one of my contacts about getting me a forty-five revolver with all the numbers wiped off, not one that had been in a dozen hold-ups.

'OK, boss, leave it to me,' the young black guy seemed pleased to have been given a problem to solve.

It was back to business, but there seemed to be more guys selling hash, Mexicans, Jamaican yardies and gangsters.

Cocaine was becoming a big problem, but I swore never to deal with coke. I remember what the old cop had told me "If you only deal in the hash the cops don't care, but if you sell cocaine or crack, we will get you sooner or later." One day I was at my bar dealing hash, I didn't need to sell the stuff myself, but I would get bored sitting around the apartment with Carla smoking hash and dancing around doing the ironing naked.

Two young, well-dressed white guys came up to me and asked,

'How much for a couple of joints,' they were strangers and didn't fit in with the area.

I felt a gun in my ribs, and one of the guys whispered,

'Let's make this nice and easy, step out the back door slowly,' I smiled, 'Sure, we don't want anybody to get shot do we.' As we stepped out the back door into the yard, I grabbed his gun and twisted it around. It went off, and the young guy shut his eyes and fell clutching his side, The other guy stood frozen, then said,

'What happened?' I replied, 'Have you a car?' he nodded. We got him up and helped him to their car parked at the back of the bar. Putting him into the back seat, he kept passing out. As his friend turned the key, I said, 'Here take the gun and remember,

he was playing with the gun when he shot himself. Accidentally, now get him to a hospital.'

I decided to let my contacts do the dealing, while I organized the business. I went to a little diamond store in downtown Los Angeles and spoke with the owner. An old guy with bad eyes and an even worse bad breath problem. I showed him one diamond. We went into his office, and he inspected the diamond with an eyeglass.

'It's a fake, but I'll give you five hundred dollars for your trouble.' I snatched the diamond out of his clenched hand; he didn't want to let go. I laughed; 'You are a crook old man.' He pressed a bell under his desk.

A door swung open, and a big fat old guy came in. The old man shouted, 'He has my diamond, take it off him.' As the big guy grabbed my neck I elbowed him in the stomach then turned around and punched him in the side of his head. Falling back against the wall I kicked him in the lower region. He doubled up and crashed to the floor. I turned around, the old man was sitting at his desk, holding a gun, and shouted, 'Give me that diamond.' I smiled and stepped to the door.

I heard a click, I looked at the old man, he was standing pointing the gun at me. He pulled the trigger again—another click! I slapped his face, and he staggered back into his chair. Taking the gun from his shaking hand and looking at the gun—the safety catch was still on! Walking out into the sunshine I took a deep breath and wondered if the old guy knew that the safety catch was on.

At the bottom of that street was another small jewellery store. The owner was a younger guy, looking more like a city trader than a shopkeeper. Waving to a chair we sat at a fancy oak-carved desk, and a girl with a smile that showed a set of stainless-steel braces brought coffee. She stepped away, did a curtsy then said with a broad grin, 'Will that be all sir?' When she had gone, the manager shook his head. Slowly stirring his coffee and staring at the diamond, he said, 'She is my sister's daughter. She wants to be an actress.'

He shook his head again. Looking at the diamond through an eyeglass for several seconds. He put the eyeglasses and the diamond on the table and opened a drawer. Pulling out a newspaper and spreading it in front of me. The headlines were all about a diamond robbery at one of the major dealers. A ten-thousand-dollar reward was offered. He waited till I had read the page, then said, 'The diamonds were never recovered. Where did this stone come from?' He paused and sat back in his chair. 'Look, I'll take the risk. One thousand dollars cash and no questions asked! I smiled and picked the diamond off the desk.

'You and I know it's worth ten times that. He leaned forward.

'OK, ok. I'll get my valuer over and offer you half of what he says. He stood and went into the front of the shop.

'I'll ring him now. Stay there and enjoy your coffee.' I opened the door an inch. He was talking on the phone with his hand cupped to the mouthpiece. I flung the door open and marched past the guy who held the phone to his chest and shouted to me, 'Wait, the valuer is on his way over.' I was a hundred yards down the street when a cop car passed and stopped at the shop.

The two cops were met at the door by the manager.

I figured, that if these diamonds were from a robbery in this city, I would have to get rid of them somewhere else. I know now why I was getting low offers; the local jewellers knew the stones were hot. I would have to find a bent diamond dealer and a money launderer who would not run off with my cash. Was I asking too much?

CHAPTER 6

I knew the guy who owned the bar, I gave him one hundred dollars every week to let me deal there. I said, 'I guess I am in trouble now.' He laughed. 'These guys try and shakedown the smaller dealers, but be careful, you have humiliated them, and word travels fast.'

I was a little paranoid for the next couple of weeks. Every Saturday, I would take Carla to lunch at an upmarket restaurant, then shopping or dancing at a late-night club. We also moved into a high-rise apartment block with views over the city, I felt a lot safer there, with a doorman on duty twenty-four hours. The gun that I took off the mafia guy, was a small pearl-handled gun, with a silencer fitted, I swopped it for my little revolver.

I was looking to expand my contacts, I interviewed one young black guy, who said that he had lost his job and that the bank was going to foreclose on his house, throwing his wife and two kids out into the street, He struck me as decent guy who had some bad luck. I gave him a small amount of hash to sell and all the contact details, he told me where he lived.

I rang a lawyer friend and asked him to find out which bank held the mortgage on the young guy's house, I went downtown to the bank that the lawyer had told me, held the loan. I asked for the loan manager and was shown into a small office, the guy sitting at the desk was a smartly dressed dude, and we got chatting over a coffee, the guy started to tell me how he had been held back from promotion by his 'Son of a bitch' manager, I made some sympathetic sounds.

I got onto the subject of the mortgage on the young contact's house. The loan guy put the papers onto his desk, and he said,

'I think we are going ahead with the eviction! it is up to my manager to make the deciding choice.' I put my hand on his shoulder, looked him in the eye and said, 'You can decide that,

'Son of a bitch' he thought for a minute, nodded then said,

'Sure, after all, I am the loan manager.'

He looked at the paperwork. 'Look If he can come up with three thousand dollars, the eviction will be cancelled and he will be a three-month mortgage ahead.' I opened my bag and put three thousand bucks onto his desk. He stared at me for a moment, then called an office girl in to count the money, he stamped a couple of documents and handed me a receipt, we shook hands then I left.

I was feeling good as I drove to Albie's house. He came to the door, come in boss, he introduced me to his wife, a thin girl holding a baby, she said sorry, but we have run out of coffee. I handed Albie a fifty-dollar note, he looked in amazement, and I quickly said

'It's an advance on your commission.'

He threw his arms around me. 'While I am here, here is another advance on your wages,' I handed his wife the mortgage document, she read it and started to weep. Albie put his arm around his sobbing wife and said, 'Anything I can do for you, just say the word. I walked out to my car feeling absolved of all my sins. Surely now the scales of good versus evil had swung back in my favour

Carla and I drove along the coast freeway to Los Angeles I wanted to see if I could expand my business into this beautiful city. We booked into a hotel overlooking the bay. Then took a walk downtown. The place was a mess, with hippies, drug addicts and guys and girls beating drums and waving tambourines blocking the walkways. This was a prime place for my goods, so I checked out some of the dealers. They were mostly hippies, raising a few dollars to buy more hash. Some of the hash was poor quality, mixed with all sorts of horse shit!

I felt that our brand of good quality products and honest dealing would win the market.

I went into a low-life bar in the Bay Area, looking for potential contacts.

I got talking with a student, who was reading a book in an alcove.

'Hi, man, I think I have found someone who could use a few bucks,' he smiled, 'What have I got to do?' I smiled back,

'Just sell a few joints around the university? he shook his head,

'I haven't any cash to lay out,'

I said, 'Don't worry about the money, just sell the stuff and we will work the money out. He said his name was Andy and he was studying for a law degree. What!

One evening, Carla opened the door of the apartment to a middle-aged couple, brought them in, and they sat down at the table, Carla made some coffee, and then the guy said, 'I need help! I am a council member on the Los Angeles council, and I am being blackmailed,' I said, 'What makes you think that I can help?' he looked at me, 'I've heard that you know everyone worth knowing.

Plus, you're a straight-up guy, and I can't go to the police.' He told me that he was at a hotel bar, and somebody spiked his drink, and he woke up on a bed, naked with a woman, and a guy filming. They threatened to send a copy of the film to my church congregation, 'I am an Elder of the church.' He put his head into his hands and sobbed, After a minute he said, 'I have access to the council safe, and they want a million dollars for the film.'

'How are they going to contact you?' I asked. He lifted his head 'They said, when you have the money, I have to ring the number that they gave me.'

He passed me a slip of paper with the name Joey, and a number. I asked, 'And what's in it for me?' the guy looked at his wife who said, 'How much do you want?' I quickly replied, 'I don't want money, but I may need a favour in the future.' He nodded,

'If you can get me out of this situation, consider it done.'

I had a friend trace the phone number to an address in the suburbs, and I drove over there. `it was a single-story clapboard house. Parking a few houses down, and walking up to the door.

Two bell rings later, and it is opened by a tall white guy with a long scar on his cheek. I gave him my best genuine smile and said,

'Hi, I am looking for the last family who lived here,' he looked me up and down, turned his head and called into the house. A young well-dressed girl came to the door and told me, 'This place was rented to an old guy, who didn't keep up with the rent so they stuck him into an old folk's home.' I wrote the information down as if it was important to me.

I phoned the councillor,

'Ring him, and tell him that you will have the money on Friday, and where you can meet him. I told him to pick a quiet wooded area, outside of town and a time to meet.

On Friday.' I filled a bag with newspapers, wore a hat and gloves, put a revolver with a silencer into my trouser belt and set off to the meeting place. Parked in a quiet spot. I didn't have to wait long. A car pulled up by the trees. In the evening dusk, I saw there were two people in the car: Knocking on the window, The guy with the scarred face wound it down, and asked, 'Got the money?' I held up the bag, and as he leaned out of the window to grab it, I shot him in the head. The girl screamed, and leaning into the car, as I shot her in the head.

Then putting the gun into the guy's hand, it took me two minutes to search his jacket pocket, I found his house keys and went back to my car.

At the clapboard house, the door was unlocked, I went in and found an office, in one of the drawers there was a camera, and some pictures of the councillor lying on the bed with a girl, it was the same girl I had just shot. And one picture of two guys lying naked on a bed. I took the motherboard out of the computer and checked there was no other film, so I tidied up and left. Locking the door, and putting the keys under a pot at the side of the door.

The next morning, I watched the news on TV. There had been four homicides last night, drug gang-related, and a murder-suicide. The next day the councillor rang. His voice quivered as he asked what happened. I told him that I had urged them to leave the country, then said, 'Do not ever ring this number again.'

The student, Andy, who was studying for a law degree? Wanted more hash. The word had got around that it was the best in Los Angeles. He said that he spent more time dealing with hash than studying to become a lawyer.

The money was piling up in the cupboard, time for another trip to Switzerland. But I was nervous, too many bad things had happened there, so I decided to go alone. I got myself another passport, but the face on the passport had a small beard, so I had to wait a couple of weeks for the beard to grow.

I decided not to fly into Zurich, in case my face was on the wanted list at the customs, I flew into Orlay in France, took the long train ride to Zurich, found a back-street bed and breakfast, cleaned up, and took a taxi to the bank. The young manager welcomed me into his office, over a coffee he said, 'You may find this interesting! He pulled a paper from a drawer, with a blurred photo of a man outside a bar, he smiled, 'He looks like you, no.? This is the guy the cops are looking for.

I took two fifty-dollar notes from my pocket, and put them on his desk, he said, 'There is no need sir,' as he slipped the notes into his pocket like a professional. We finished the coffee and then banked the money, the manager gave me his office phone number and said,

'It might be prudent to call me first before you visit again.' Taking a taxi back to the bed and breakfast, as we turned into the street. Through the windscreen, I saw two police cars at the door. Tapping the driver on his shoulder, I said, 'I've changed my mind, take me to the airport' He nodded and drove past the police cars and onto the airport. Back in my apartment in Los Angeles, Carla gave me a note with a number, he asked me if you would ring him. I rang the number, and a guy said, 'Hello, is that George?'

I took a mouthful of coffee and said, 'What do you want?' He told me that his dad had just died, and left some money to his brother, his uncle, who was in the Los Angeles Men's Central Prison for the past twenty-two years for murder. He had been a hitman for the mob. He told me that his dad had left some money to his uncle and would go to jail and tell him of his windfall. I felt a little sorry for the guy, and besides, I was curious I had never met a hitman.

At the jail, they frisked me, then showed me into a room, airy with windows that had no bars. I thought, do they know that this guy is a mob hitman? The door opened and in shuffled a little white-haired old man, with a nurse holding his arm. She helped him into the chair and helped him put his glasses on. He looked at me, and in a croaky voice said, 'Have you brought me chocolate?'

Looking at the nurse, she handed me a small bar of chocolate.

'Here pop, here's your chocolate.'

He was dribbling down his chin. I took a good look at him.

The engine was running, but no one was driving! I explained to the nurse that his brother had died and the rest of the message that his nephew had told me.

The nurse shook her head, smiled, and whispered; 'I'll tell him, but he will forget two minutes later, he can't remember his name.'

I found a wall phone on the way out and rang his nephew and told him that the old boy was in good health, and asking about him, he was saying that he was going to meet you when he gets out in another ten years' time.'

The nephew thanked me, and said, 'I work on an oil platform but when I get back to Kansas, I'll give the relatives the good news'.

Another good deed is done; I will go to heaven after all.

CHAPTER 7

The doorman from my apartment building, told Carla, that a couple of guys were caught on the CTC camera, in the parking area, trying to get into the boot of my car. I delivered a lot of the hash to my contacts in the car boot, plus, I would put the bundles of cash in there, maybe somebody was following me.

I went to the garage of a customer, called Filipe after I told him that I wanted a break-in proof boot, he patted my arm, winked, and said, 'For you my friend, consider it done.' I got the car back the next day, he had welded steel plates to make a box, and the lid of the boot had a combination and a key lock, he also fitted an alarm.

We sat at the back of the garage in his little office that stank of diesel and had a beer. He told me that the city council was closing down his garage because he didn't have all the right paperwork for the fire regs. I liked the look of Filipe. He seemed a genuine guy. I tapped his arm with my beer can and smiled,

'I might be able to help Amigo.'

I rang the Los Angeles councillor whom I had helped out and explained that a friend of mine had a problem with his paperwork.

He whispered into the phone,

'I don't know if I can do anything.' Taking a deep breath I growled, 'Were you the guy who was being blackmailed, and you needed my help, the same guy who was afraid that his congregation might find out his dirty little secret?

Get off your fat ass and sort it.' Then slammed the phone down. A week later I popped into the garage to pay the bill, and Filipe took me into his office for a beer. Filipe held up some documents.

'Look Amigo! Two days after you left the garage, these documents were handed to me by a middle-aged, office-looking guy, he asked my name, gave me the papers, and marched out.'

'I said, 'Gee, was it Santa Claus?' and smiled,

Filipe put his head to one side, smiled and said,

'Did you fix this?' I tried to look serious and replied,

'I am not the mayor!'

On Friday I returned from doing business, and on the kitchen table was a letter, it was from Carla, it read, "Dearest George, I've taken a little money from the cupboard, and I am going home to London. It has not been as much fun as when we were bumming around the grape farm with the hippies, it is too dangerous when you have to take a gun with you when you leave the apartment, you know where to find me, if you come back to London, love and kisses, Carla."

I sat at the table in silence. It was getting dark outside, but I didn't put the lights on. I poured myself a large Johnnie Walker and tried to think! I had over a million dollars stashed here, and around the world, is it time to bail out and return to London? I got drunk and collapsed into the empty bed. I drove around to Felipe's garage with the excuse that the boot lid was sticking. He took me into his office, 'What's wrong, Hombre?' I poured out my problems, and he laughed, 'I wish that I had your problems.' He patted my arm,

'It's my brother's birthday this evening.' He gave me the address, 'It would be an honour to have you come and meet my family, because of you, I still have a garage,' he winked.

I bought a cowboy hat as a gift to his brother, and a bunch of flowers in case he had a wife. I found the address and parked up. Mexican guitar and trumpet music was coming from the house. Felipe saw me and pulled me into the room that was packed with people, young, old, grandads, grandmas, teenagers and kids. I had to shake hands with everyone. I gave his younger brother the cowboy hat, and his wife the flowers. I stepped out into the yard for air. Some guys were smoking hash and speaking in Spanish. They waved, and I waved back. A girl came up to me and held out a beer.

I took the beer and said thanks,

then she took out a pack of cigarettes, and I shook my head, 'No thanks,' She hesitated and held the cigarette in the air.

'Do you mind if I?' She looked at me between puffs.

'Do you speak Spanish?' I smiled, 'It takes all my time to speak English.' She laughed and said, 'My name is Marri, and yours,'

'Santa!' She smiled, 'As in Santa Clause?'

Marri was about nineteen, with tanned skin and long thick black hair with beautiful white teeth. She told me that she was attending the University of Los Angeles, studying chemistry. She said she had just broken up with her boyfriend because she had caught him using cocaine.

With the noise of the music, I couldn't hear. I said, 'Marri, I know a nice quiet bar, want to come?' she smiled,

'OK. But first, I have to say goodbye to my family.' Felipe came over to say goodbye, he whispered, 'Be careful Amigo, she has two very tough brothers,' then winked.

We sat at the bar on plush seats and got into deep conversation. Marri turned out to be something of an intellectual! That was something that turned me on! An intelligent woman who could hold a subject with interesting ideas. After an hour, and with a little too much to drink. Marri helped me out of the bar to a taxi, and she got in with me. At the apartment, Marri made coffee,

'A nice place you have, where is your wife?' I muttered,

'Who would stick me,' she laughed,

'No girlfriend?' I leaned over the table and flattened a photo of Carla. 'Nope.' Sipping the coffee, she paused, 'Are you gay?'

I showed Marri around the apartment, in the bedroom I put my arms around her and kissed that lovely mouth, and she kissed me back. I put my hand around her back and slowly pulled the zip down. She started to pull away, then paused, closed her eyes, and pushed into me. The dress fell to the floor.

In the morning, she made coffee and got back into bed. She kissed me and said, 'Well, that's the gay theory gone,'

we both laughed and finished our coffee, I kissed her and said,

'Maybe we should test out that theory again?'

Marri dressed. We took a taxi to pick up my car, Marri said,

'If I am not in the lecture hall in one hour, I'll miss my class?' We drove to the university. She kissed me, and smiling said,

'We may have to test out that theory again soon.'

As I entered the apartment the phone was ringing, it was Moe, 'George I am in jail, but I'll send the big guy over to pick up the money, same place, same time.' That didn't sound like Moe, he would chat away about anything and everything.

I had a bundle of cash to give to Moe. I felt uneasy about giving it to the big guy! I arrived at the meeting place well in advance, parked the car out of sight, and hid in the shadows, I checked the gun in my pocket and the little derringer in my sock.

The Cadillac pulled up with the big guy in the driving seat. In the dusk, I saw another guy sit up from the back seat, and then duck down just as fast.

The big guy got out of the car and lit a cigarette, I stepped out of the shadows, and said, 'Hi, where is Moe?'

The back door of the car flew open, and a little black guy with a bandana around his head pointed a sawn-off shotgun at me,

I put my hands up, 'Take it easy man!

The big guy said, 'Don't move or make any sounds, that shotgun has a hair-trigger.' They both laughed.

The big guy patted me down and took my gun from my trouser belt. He stared at me and said, mockingly. 'Do you want to speak to Moe?' He pushed me to the back of the caddy and opened the boot. Crouching inside was Moe bound up with grey tape, his mouth was taped, and his face was bruised and covered in blood. The big guy said, 'Times are changing buddy.' The little guy with the shotgun said, 'Yeah! They sure are,' and broke into a girlish giggle.

He closed the boot, then the big guy said, 'Where is the money you brought for Moe, or should I say me!' They both laughed.

'It isn't far, I said. But look, why can't we do business? I don't care who supplies me.' The big guy paused for a moment, then nodded, 'OK. But It's money upfront from now on. I shook my head. 'Yes, that sounds fine by me, I said, but will you tell your friend to lower the shotgun, he makes me nervous.' As he lowered the gun, I bent down to my ankle pulled out my Derringer and shot him in the neck. I had practised this move many times.

Grabbing the shotgun as he fell to the ground. The big guy struggled to pull a gun from his pocket. The blast from the shotgun made him stagger back before he collapsed against the car, and slid down in slow motion.

I opened the boot and smiled at Moe as I lifted him out.

'Welcome back to the living buddy,' I got him into the back seat of the Cadillac, ripped the tape off, cleaned him up, and said,

'Look Moe, we can't hang around here with two dead bodies, the cops patrol this area, if you can drive follow me to my apartment, he nodded.

Back at my apartment, he took a shower, I gave him some clothes to change, and then we sat down to coffee. His fist banged the table. Then he stood and walked around the room shouting,

'Those bastards beat me to find my contact for the hash, you saved my life.' He reached over the table and kissed my hand then wept and said, 'I made a good choice. I knew I could trust you, right from the beginning. I made him up a bed on the sofa.

The next morning, I made coffee and breakfast, over breakfast Moe said, 'I owe you my life, what can I do for you?' I put my hand on his shoulder and smiling said, 'Nothing my friend, but I may ask a favour in the future, he held my hand and squeezed tight, saying,

'Anything, anything. I'll have your shipment of hash delivered tomorrow.' He slid into the Cadillac driver's seat. I put my hand up to stop him from speaking, and said, I have a bundle of cash to give you from the last shipment. He leaned out of the Cadillac window.

'Keep it, it is yours with my blessing.' He waved and was gone.

Marri was in the kitchen cooking; her schoolbooks were all over the table and sofa, when the doorbell rang, and two big Mexican guys were pushing their way in, one guy said, 'Where is that whore?' The other guy took a swing at me, I parried his hand and punched him on the chin, and he dropped to the floor.

The first one managed to punch me on the side of the head, and I dropped, dazed. I could hear Marri screaming at them, I struggled to stand up when he punched me again, knocking me out.

When I came too, the room was empty. My head was throbbing and my chin was bruised. Marri's books were scattered over the floor, I cleaned up and made coffee when the bell went again. I took my gun out of the cupboard and opened the door, Marri fell into my arms sobbing, she blurted out, 'That was one of my brothers and my ex-boyfriend, they are also workmates.

Marri got her things from her sister's house and moved in, I spoke with the doorman, about if those guys returned, get the cops, and ring me. I slipped a twenty-dollar note into his hand, and he saluted. I wasn't happy with Marri moving in, not with the business that I was in! But she was a great cook—if you liked Mexican food!

Every day the phone would ring for Marri, and she would shout and swear down the phone in part English and part Spanish. Sometimes she would sob after the calls. She told me that it was her mother or one of her sisters who were calling her a whore, and that the menfolk in the Spanish community was calling her a slut! Her mother said, 'That she would never find a good husband if his parents found out that she was shacking up with a Gringo.'

One Sunday we were in bed, I was reading the local paper and Merri was drawing circles on my belly when she said,

'Hey, What's this, she pushed me onto my side and said, look, you have a mole in the shape of a heart, that's strange' Then she went to shower, got dressed and went off to church.

I drove out to see Albi, the young black guy, with the skinny wife, who once told me, "Anything I can do for your boss"

When I sorted out his mortgage problem.

We sat down over coffee, and I explained that I had to go out of town on business trips from time to time, and needed someone I could trust to carry on delivering the hash to my contacts,

and collecting the money. He said, 'You can trust me, boss, I owe you a favour.'

That Friday, I took him with me to meet all my contacts, and to explain to them that he would pick up the cash if I wasn't around, then I showed him how to get into the boot of the car, dismantle the alarm, and where to park at the apartment. He looked puzzled,

'What do I do if there is a problem?' I put my hand up,

'Don't worry I'll sort the problems out when I return, and remember to count the cash!

The doorman rang up and told me that two plain-clothed cops wanted to speak to me.

They came in and sat at the table, while I made coffee. I asked,

'Now gents how can I help you,' the ugly one said,

'You can start with a thousand bucks each, I smiled, and said, 'And what do I get for my money? The ugly one leaned over.

'You avoid going to jail for the next twenty years, they looked at each other, and the other one said, 'Or maybe longer.'

43

He took out a sheet of paper and spread it out on the table. It had most of the names and addresses of my contacts. The ugly one rolled the paper up and said, 'So, it'll be two thousand a week to stay out of jail, okay sunny Jim.' I pretended to consider the offer for a moment, then said, 'Yeah, that sounds reasonable! They high-fived each other. When they had calmed down, the ugly one said,

'We will come round Saturday morning, have the money ready, they left saying, 'Saturday morning. Sunny Jim.'

I contacted Billy, an ex-private detective to come over, I told him I needed some evidence on film, and he looked around the room, '

'OK give me a couple of hours, I'll be back with a friend.'

I was sweating, if I got this wrong, I could end up in jail, or be out of pocket every week, then what if they wanted more?—Help!

Billy and a young Chinese guy came back with a couple of bags of drills, cables and a video recorder. Billy sat drinking beer, while the Chinese guy removed a vent and installed a video camera and mike. Then he set up a video recorder on top of some drawers.

Finally, he sat down and wiped his brow. Glanced around and said, 'I'll have that coffee now.' Over coffee, he explained how to work everything, and where the guys had to sit, I said, 'Will the camera get the right angles? The Chinese guy said, 'I work in the porn industry. Angles are my thing.'

We burst out laughing. I paid them well. and said, 'I might need you again.'

On Saturday morning I was a bag of nerves, this had to go right the first time. The cops arrived early, and they sat on the chairs that I had carefully arranged, and asked, 'OK guys, tell me again, it's a thousand bucks, right?'

The ugly guy snarled, 'Don't play games, sunny Jim, or we will double the amount, you want to stay out of jail, right?' After we finished coffee, I took out two thousand dollars and put it on the table. It was snatched up, their eyes lit up, and they were smiling. The ugly one said, 'Don't forget sunny Jim, next Saturday, same time, same amount, they left laughing. I rang downstairs to the doorman, 'Send them up again, say that I need to speak about the money.'

When I let them in, they were still smiling. I waved them to sit. 'Guys, isn't your new police commissioner having an anti-corruption drive?' They looked puzzled when I said,? 'Maybe I should send him this.' I pushed the videotape button, and there they were, demanding money or else! The ugly guy stood up and pulled out his gun,

'I'll kill you, son of a bitch! the other guy looked miserable, and leaned back into his chair, shook his head and said,

'What are you going to do? His ugly friend stared as I said,

'First, put the money back on the table, the one with the gun pulled the tape out of the recorder, I smiled,

'You can keep that one, I'll keep the other dozen copies. They put the money back onto the table and sat in silence. I said,

'If I am going to save you bums from jail, you will have to do me a favour, sometime in the future? Right guys,' they both nodded, now get your corrupt asses out of my apartment, bye, bye, sunny Jim.'

I poured myself a large Johnnie Walker, while my heart rate returned to normal! I suddenly realised that was the only copy! There was a knock on the door, and I put my gun into my belt, have the cops figured out that was the only copy? I opened the door and there was Marri's mother and two of her sisters.

They brushed past me and sat down. The mother had tears on her cheeks, she took my hand, and said, 'You are ruining my daughter's chances of finding a husband, please, if you are a good man.' I weakened, they looked so sad. 'OK, get her things from the bedroom, and her books, The mother's face broke into a wide grin as she suddenly produced shopping bags, and filled them with Marri's clothes and books. When they had the bags full, she kissed me on the cheek. The youngest sister went to hug me. Her mother pushed her away and growled at her in Spanish. Then turned to me and said,

'All my daughters are sluts.' The two girls grinned. I gave the mum twenty bucks for a taxi and waved them goodbye.

Moe was always asking me to come down to his house in Florida, and I needed a break from all the drama, so I locked up, and gave my car keys to Albi, then got him to drive me to LA. Airport.

On the flight to Miami, I started to relax and fell asleep. I was awakened by the wheels skipping on the tarmac. Moe, and a young lady, met me at the Airport in his black Cadillac.

The sun was blazing, and the heat was stifling.

I sat in the back with Moe, who kept patting my shoulder and said,

45

'Now I am going to show you a good time, my friend.'

Moe's house was facing the beachfront. An enormous modern mansion with six bedrooms, six bathrooms and a pool at the back, Moe smiled as he said, 'You bought me this.' Monica, the young girl showed me to my room. Putting my shorts on I walked out of the house to the pool. Took a swim in the cool water, and when I got out, Monica brought me a bottle of black-label Johnnie Walker, crystal glass and a bowl of ice cubes. We sat under a huge parasol on a tiled patio Moe's girl, Monica, sat at the table, she was *almost* wearing a bikini. She told me that Moe paid her a hundred bucks a day to look good for when he had guests around the house, she told me that she was married with a kid, that her mother was looking after. I took a sip of the golden nectar, 'Where is your husband? She said,

'He's abroad in the military, she laughed, when he comes home, I am the sweet wife, gingham dresses and ribbons in my hair, cooking in the kitchen. As soon as he goes back abroad, she smiled, I am a hundred bucks a day, half-naked waitress in Moe's house.'

We both laughed, when she said, 'I love it here.'

Moe seemed to be on the phone for hours at a time, but I didn't mind, I relaxed, played tennis, drank whisky in the cool evenings, and often had a game of cards with Monica.

One evening, I was having a late-night swim to relieve the heat of the day, when there was a splash as someone dived into the pool behind me, I turned around and it was Monica,.. minus her bikini. She kissed me, and said, 'Moe said to keep you happy.'

I put my arms around her, 'Monica my lovely, you have got me smiling already.'

It came to the end of the week too soon. I had a long talk with Moe about business and money and enjoyed the charms and nights with the lovely Monica. On the way back to the airport, Monica drove to let Moe and I discuss business. He took my hand,

'You saved my life. I'll never forget that.

Remember, if there is anything, I can do for you.' Putting his head on my shoulder. 'Don't get emotional,' I said, 'This is a new shirt.

In the waiting lounge we had a drink at the bar, Moe said,

'Why don't you come and live here in Florida, a guy with money could live like a king down here, and you can still do business,'

I put my hand on his shoulder and looked over at Monica.

'Don't tempt me.' She smiled.

When I arrived at LA International it was raining and dull, I couldn't help comparing it to the endless sunshine I had just left. Albi met me with a handshake and drove me home parked up looked around opened the car boot, and took a large kit bag up to the apartment. Over a coffee, Albi gave me the news, then threw the bag onto the sofa. As he opened the bag, I said, 'What are you doing Albi? The bag was jammed with cash.

'Aren't you going to count the money? He said.

'But I trust you Albi! Why should I count the cash? He smiled, 'Thanks, boss.'

I drove to Felipe's garage, sitting in his office with a beer, he told me that Merri was back living with her sister, and she was engaged to a fellow student, a guy from a good Mexican family, with prospects! I knew that her mother would be happy, he told me that Merri and her classmates were going to celebrate their graduation on Saturday night at a Mexican nightclub. I wished that he hadn't told me that news.

On Saturday night I had an urge to see Merri one last time! Driving to the club and parking at the back. I strolled past the door, peering in, as I walked slowly past.

Some girls came out for air and smoke and chattered loudly. I took a deep breath and walked into the club. Standing by the bar and asking myself, what the hell am I thinking, not daring to look at the dance floor, there was a huge mirror behind the bar wall. Peering at the crowd, the place was mobbed and I could not make anyone out.

Feeling a little guilty for even being there I decided to finish my drink and get out. As I took the last sip, I felt a tap on my shoulder, I slowly put my glass on the bar and turned around.

Merri reached up and kissed me. Without speaking she took my hand and led me out of the club. The nearest hotel was a short walk away. We booked in, went upstairs, undressed and got into bed. We kissed long and hard. Merri said,

'This is the last time we can meet. I am getting married to a good man who loves me. She reached up and kissed me, But for now, let's not think about that.'

In the morning I sent her home in a taxi,

'Where will you say you have been? She smiled; 'My sister owes me a big favour.' I went back to the apartment to count the money that Albi had delivered. It was correct down to the last dollar. The money was piling up at the apartment.

It was time for another trip, I rang Moe and told him that I had to go and hide some money, and my hiding place was Switzerland.

'Why go to Switzerland?' He asked. 'I can introduce you to some investors down here in Miami, who will give you a good return for your money?' I said, 'Is it the Mafia?' Moe laughed,

'No, it is some developers, they will give you some deeds of other property as security I have some investments with them myself. I decided to give that a try as I would feel more comfortable on home territory, so to speak. I hadn't forgotten there was still an arrest warrant waiting for me in Switzerland.

I flew to Miami and met with Moe. I took a bag with one million dollars, Moe told me he had set up a meeting with a couple of investors, at his house, I looked around, but couldn't see Monica. Moe smiled, 'Her husband's come home, Sorry.'

On the day of the meeting, Moe got a call telling him the venue had changed. We drove to a plush hotel overlooking the beach and went up to a stateroom, sitting at the table were three guys, one old guy with a silver beard, and wearing dark glasses, the other two were younger. We shook hands all around then Moe said, 'Gents let me introduce you to my brother, the old guy chuckled, 'Has he lost his tan?' Moe ignored the remark and said, 'I consider this guy to be my Brother, he saved my life.'

One of the young guys spoke.

'My father is looking for an investment of two million dollars.' the old boy nodded, and I said, 'Well, that counts me out, the best that I would invest is a million, and only with guarantees, and what's the return?' The old guy tapped on the table, cleared his throat and said, 'We will take your million for a five per cent return! I laughed; 'I can get that return from the post office. The three guys huddled together and whispered, the old guy asked,

'What kind of return are you looking for?' I whispered to Moe, 'What shall I ask for? He whispered try ten per cent! I looked at the old guy.

'Twelve per cent,' the old guy smiled. Cleared his throat again, 'Ten per cent,' I looked at Moe, who shrugged.

48

'If I agree, what guarantees do I get?' A briefcase was put on the table, and one of the young guys pulled out a bunch of house deeds and handed me two of the deeds. The young guy said, 'These two properties are worth over two million,' I looked at Moe, and he nodded. There was a moment of silence. I said, 'Let me check out these deeds first, we can meet here tomorrow, same time. Everyone nodded. The old guy cleared his throat.

I left with Moe and drove to Moe's lawyer's office, the lawyer sat us down in some plush red leather chairs, I showed him the deeds, he put his glasses on and inspected the documents, after a moment, he picked up the phone and spoke for a couple of minutes, then he handed me back the deeds.

He took his glasses off, and said, 'These are all in order, this office has dealt with one of the properties, it is clear of the mortgage, just get the guy to sign in front of a witness, and these two houses are yours, I would be glad to assist if you wish?' I looked at him,

'How about being the witness?

I told him the address and time, he looked at his diary,

'Yes, I'll be there.'

We all sat down at the hotel, the old guy signed the papers, and then the lawyer did his signing, I asked the lawyer to look after the papers, and he agreed, and wrote out a receipt then he signed it, and handed it to me, I then handed over the bag with a million dollars, one of the young guys tipped the money out onto the table, and both guys started counting. I went back to Moe's house,

'Is this all kosher? Moe nodded then said, 'I have been dealing with this family for years, and I have always got my investment back, plus interest, I had invested several million at one time and used that same lawyer to do the paperwork, and it all went smoothly, also, he knows how to hide the cash from prying eyes.' I spent another couple of days with Moe, swimming, playing tennis, drinking whisky and relaxing. Time seemed to pass quickly, and it was then time to go to the Airport. Moe asked, 'Have you given it any thought about moving down here? I shook my head. 'Unfortunately, I need to work.'

It was nearly seven months since Merri got married, I was strolling down the main street on Saturday. When, coming towards me, was Merri, and her husband, pushing a pram. We stopped to talk, and Marri introduced me to Marco, her husband, we shook hands, and Merri looked at Marco, and said, 'George is a friend of Felipe,' Merri took the baby out of the pram to show me, I said,

'What a lovely child,' to Marco. Merri pulled the shawl off the baby, and said, 'Look, the baby has a mole on his hip in the shape of a heart, she smiled, isn't that strange?' I nodded and Marco shrugged.

The money was piling up again. Deliveries were coming in regularly. There was the odd problem with my dealers getting hassle from bums, and would-be tough guys.

I had done a deal with an old ex-prize fighter, who had fallen on hard times. He would sort out any guys that bothered my contacts, and in return, I would pay off his bar bill and slip him a few bucks. I would have a drink with him now and then.

He would tell me stories about his fights. He told me that sometimes, he had to take a dive, to win a bet. Back in his day, crooks ran the fight business.

CHAPTER 8

Carla would often come into my thoughts. I decided to take a trip to London, so I arranged for Albi to look after things. I arrived at Heathrow in the middle of a rainstorm, I had forgotten about the British weather. Taking a taxi to Maida-vale, it was getting late, so I booked into a small hotel on Kilburn Road. After a shower and a change of warmer clothes. Guys and gals were still wearing T-shirts and shorts in the rain. I forgot how hardy the Brits were.!

Taking a stroll along a familiar street and passing the Empire.

I went into a bar that I used to frequent many years ago. The Rifle. On Kilburn High Street, they served the best Guinness in London. It was good to hear familiar voices again. I stayed a little too late, got drunk and was thrown out at closing time. Staggered out of the bar, into the cold air, I also forgot, how cold it got in London.

The next morning, all spick and span, I stepped out into the cool morning air, such a difference from the blistering heat of LA. I ate breakfast at a café on the high road, and read the local paper, it started to feel like home again. Waving a taxi down and showed the driver the strip of paper with Carla's address. The cabbie glanced at the address, flicked a cigarette butt into the gutter, and said,

'You could have walked it in two minutes Matey.' The street was a quarter a mile away!

I knocked on the door, and Carla opened the door with a child in her arms, 'George,' she smiled, 'Come in. Putting the child into a crib, made coffee, and sat. She looked at the child and said,

'I met an old boyfriend when I got back home. We clicked and got married. Then she patted her stomach and said, 'Number two on the way!' We both laughed. She looked at the clock on the wall, 'He will be arriving home soon,' she smiled again,

'I don't know how to explain you away, do you mind?' she kissed me at the door, and said, 'We had fun back then but this is my life now.'

I stayed a couple of days, taking in all the familiar places, and visited the bar where Carla and I lived, before going hiking around Europe. I had a drink with one of the barmen, who still worked there, and he remembered me. I got a little sentimental,

'Any chance of getting my job and room back,' we both laughed. I was a broke kid back then and now I was a millionaire.

I waved goodbye to London and boarded the plane for LA. As the jet lifted into the sky above London I wondered if I would ever see the place again. Several hours later I got off at the LA airport, the sun was dazzling and the temperature was in the nineties. I took a cab back to the apartment, and rang Albi, to check that all was well. His first words were, 'Got some money for you, boss.' Then Albi told me that he had moved to the suburbs.

I drove over to Alibi's new address, a typical suburban detached house, with a white picket fence at the front, and a car in the driveway. Alibi's skinny wife showed me into the lounge and gave me coffee. As she put the cup down, she grinned and said,

'Thanks to you we can afford the best coffee.' Albi came in from the backyard, wearing gardening gloves, gardening trousers and green slip-on shoes. He looked like a typical suburban dweller.

He shook my hand, 'Let me show you around the house,' Upstairs, Albi pulled a rug sack from a cupboard,

'Here is your money with the lists of customers, boss.' I said,

'Albi, you are practically running the whole show now, cos I need to take a little time out to sort out some of my affairs.'

Downstairs, Albie's skinny wife was looking for non-existing dust, with a feather duster. I took the bag of money and drove back to the apartment.

The phone rang, it was the lawyer from Miami, 'Got some bad news...Moe is dead! I held my breath for a moment.

My head was spinning. Moe was dead. The lawyer went on, 'He was found floating in the pool, with a bullet in his head.

The cops said, that it looked like a professional hit.' I said, 'I will be down to Miami as fast as I can.

I rang Albi and told him to take over, and that I would be gone for a while, I caught the first flight down to Miami. It's a five-hour flight from LA to Miami, so I had plenty of time to get my thoughts together, maybe if I had moved down to Miami like Moe said, this would not have happened, l could not believe that Moe was dead.

As I sat in the lawyer's plush chair, he had a pile of papers on his huge desk, he said a girl called Monica, saw the gunman shoot Moe, as he was taking his usual morning swim, she hid in a bedroom and called the cops.

The lawyer picked up a paper, put on his glasses, and said, Moe left his entire estate to you! 'What?' I gasped, and the lawyer picked up another letter and went on, he stated in this letter, that he owes you his life, and that you were the only guy that didn't try and cheat him in your business dealings.

He has left you his house, the Cadillac, and these two safety deposit keys, Moe wrote in this letter, that you would know the numbers to get into the boxes.

I took the keys and went in a cab to Moe's house. A cop was standing at the door. No one was allowed in.

Monica came out of the front door, wearing a black dress, and spoke to the cop, 'He is a business friend of the deceased,' she took me into the kitchen, and we sat down with a coffee, Monica told me that she was tidying up in the lounge when she looked out of the glass sliding doors and saw a guy with a gun shoot Moe, then saw her watching him and started to walk to the house. She ran into a bedroom and called the cops.

Would you recognize the gunman if you saw him again? Monica thought for a moment, 'Sure, he was a tall white guy,
a shaved head, and with a tattoo of a swan on his neck.'

I told Monica that Moe had left me the house and that I would pay her to look after things until I decided what I was going to do, she smiled, 'Of course, Moe helped me out of a jam, I owe him, God rest his soul.'

We went upstairs, to Moe's bedroom. Monica showed me a wall safe behind a mirror, it had a numbered combination. I tried a couple of numbers off my head, but no luck, I sat on Moe's bed looking at the safe.

Then, I remembered Moe telling me about his time in the army, over a few drinks one night, he laughed and showed me a tattoo on his shoulder, it was his army number. While Monica was downstairs getting me a glass of whisky, I put Moe's army number into the digits.

Bingo! I opened the safe, there was a couple of thousand dollars, some papers and a pearl-handled revolver, with a silencer fitted, I stuck the gun into my trouser belt, took out a couple of hundred bucks, and closed the safe. Monica came in with my whisky,

'Any luck?' I shook my head.

I drove the Cadillac down to police headquarters and spoke with a detective, who came into the office, he was carrying a plastic cup of coffee, and a doughnut, as he drank his coffee, he said,

'Now sir, how can I help?' I explained that I was looking for a long-lost, army buddy, the cop asked, through a mouthful of a doughnut, 'Have you got a picture?' Shaking my head.

'No, but I can give you a pretty good description!' He smiled, 'Sorry, we are not allowed to show pictures of potential faces.'

'I think this might help you to help find me, my old army buddy. I put a hundred-dollar bill on his desk! He quickly snatched it. 'Well, if it was for an old buddy,'

He pushed the coffee away and threw the doughnut into the waste bin. switched his computer on. I gave him the description that Monica had described, and he started to scroll through faces with tattoos, he stopped at the face of a guy with a swan tattoo on his neck, the guy had a shaved head. He leaned back and said,

'This guy is a bad hombre! He has a criminal sheet as long as my arm, are you sure that you want to meet this guy?' He gave me an address and said good luck with this one. I drove over to the address. It was a rough part of town.

A little guy with a bandage around his arm opened the door. I said that I was looking for the guy with the tattoo.

He came through from the kitchen, pointing a shotgun at me, he was a mean-looking dude, and he snarled, 'What do you want?' I said that I was told you were the man to speak to if I wanted someone dead. They both burst out laughing, the guy spoke to the little fella with the bandage,

'Search him for a wire. He patted me down and pulled out the pearl-handled revolver, and the money. Putting it on the table. 'Look, man, I said, Why don't we sit down, and I'll put a proposition to you!' We all sat in the kitchen. The guy said, 'Here, take some of this money and fetch some Coke.' The little guy snatched the money and went to the door.

'By the way, what's your name,' I said, 'Santa. As in Santa Claus.'

I heard the front door close; the guy kept the shotgun pointed 'What's the proposition then?' I started to speak when the front door opened, and the little guy came in and put a tiny bag of white powder on the table, and a pack of beers into the fridge.

They both spread the coke out on the table and started to sniff it up their noses. The shotgun was laid on the table, my gun was in front of the big guy, I shouted, 'Hey, do you mind if I get myself a beer?' They didn't answer, they seemed to engrossed with the Coke. I slowly stood and crept to the fridge. I looked around at the table as I moved slowly.

They were busy sniffing the coke, I leaned over and grabbed my revolver. Shooting the little guy in the head. As he dropped to the floor, the big guy looked surprised and grabbed the shotgun,

I pressed my gun into his neck, and he slowly let go of the shotgun, then laughed as he looked at the white powder on the table.

'Mind if I finish? While he carried on sniffing the Coke, I took the shotgun off the table. He seemed to be more interested in finishing the Coke than in his dead friend stretched on the floor. Finally, he leaned back in his chair, there was white powder all over his nose and cheeks. He smiled and asked, 'What do you want?' I sat on the other side of the table; 'You killed a good friend of mine! He smiled, I pointed the gun, 'Who paid you? He put his hands behind his head, 'If I told you who, I would be a dead man in days,' I smiled, 'If you don't tell me, you will be a dead man in minutes.'

"Look, how about this? I'll give you twice what you got paid to kill Moe, you will be able to hide out and fill your nose with Coke, I will even give you my revolver to take for protection.' He was silent for a moment, the Coke was beginning to take effect, He closed his eyes, and seemed to be talking to himself,

'I have always wanted to see New York, are you serious Santa? 'Look, give me the name of the guy who paid you, and you are on your way to New York with a load of cash! He opened his eyes.

'OK, Santa, I am going to trust you, it was a guy whom I met in a bar, a smartly dressed dude. He told me that he was holding a million dollars for a client, that he didn't want to give back,' I said, 'Describe him' He described Moe's lawyer down to his shoes, the one guy that Moe said that I could trust. The guy seemed awake. 'Are you going to get me that money? He stood up, and I handed him back his shotgun, as I went to the door, he said, 'Sorry man,' I turned around, and he was pointing the shotgun at me, 'Goodbye Santa,' and pulled the trigger, there was a click, he looked at me with his mouth open, I took two shotgun shells from my pocket, threw then on the table, then shot him in the head.

It was late as I waited in the basement car park, the lawyer came out of the lift and went to a white Lincoln Continental, I pulled my mask down as I crept behind him and put the gun into his back, he put his hands in the air and said, 'Take my wallet, but there isn't much, sorry,' he smiled. pressing the gun into his back,

'Let's go back to your office.

We stepped into the lift, I saw a camera pointing at us as we went into his office, he sat down and said, 'I know it's you Santa, is this a hold-up?' I took off the mask. 'I know that it was you who had Moe killed,' he smiled again, 'That might be a problem to prove, without a confession, I pointed the gun and said, 'I don't want a confession, just open that safe,' he said,

'Now why should I do that?

'Because if you don't, I will shoot you! But I'll give you a better deal than you gave Moe, I'll take half of the million that you stole, and walk away, if not; I'll kill you and nobody gets anything,' he put his finger to his lips, 'Yes, I suppose half is better than nothing.

He went to a portrait on the wall, swung it open, and there was a safe, it was full of money and documents, I handed him a bag, and he started to stuff money into the bag, I said, 'I thought you made a good living as it was?' He smiled as he put the money into the bag,

'I love the racetrack, the casino, and the painted ladies. Slow horses and fast women! I need lots of money for that. There, that's half,' I put the gun to his neck,

'Put it all in, He stopped smiling, 'But you said,'

'I lied' He put the rest of the money in the bag and growled, 'I have a lot of contacts in this town, some owe me big time, you will never live long enough to spend this money, I'll make a couple of calls, and you are a walking dead man.' He was still speaking, as I shot him in the head, I closed the safe and pulled my mask on.

I went down in the lift and peered toward the security desk, an old fat guy was snoring in his chair, surrounded by monitors, and most of the lights were out, I crept to the security desk, found the recorder, and pulled out three tapes, hoping that one of them was the recording of the lawyer and me getting into the lift.

The next day at the house, I was glued to the morning TV. It was all over the channels, a top-shot lawyer, robbed and murdered, and all the cameras in the office were down, the cops were questioning the security guard.

I put the million dollars, and his gun into Moe's safe, then drove to the bank, I showed the manager the paperwork, and he took me down to the vault with the security deposit boxes, he took out two large metal boxes and put them on a table, he handed me a buzzer 'When you want to leave, just buzz.'

He left and closed the door, I found the key to fit one of the boxes, it fitted, but to open it I had to put in a number. I sat for a moment; I'll try Moe's army number again! It worked, in the box was a pile of seven certificates, each one for one million dollars, I sat down and thought of Moe's, generosity, and wept.

I opened the other box, there were five hundred thousand dollars, and some army photos of Moe in uniform. I left the certificates in the first box and locked it. I stuffed everything from the second box, into my bag, and pressed the buzzer.

Back at the house, the cop had gone, and Monica had the pool boy change the pool water. I sat outside by the pool with a bottle of Johnnie Walker, a glass of ice, and my thoughts. Monica said,

'There are a couple of cops at the door, shall I show them in? They sat down, one of them said, looking at the bottle of whisky, 'Celebration? I lifted my glass, and took a gulp,

'Yes, to a great guy. The older cop pulled out a notebook,

'We would like to ask you about the murder of a lawyer, 'I think that you knew him,' I nodded, taking a sip of my drink,

'When last did you see him? I looked at the cops,

'Do I need a lawyer, am I a suspect, The older guy said,

'No sir, but we have to speak to anyone that knew him, do you know of any guys that might want to harm him?

'Yes, half of Miami,'

they both laughed, and they got up to leave, 'Thank you, sir. You won't leave Miami without telling us?

Monica sat with a coffee, and said, 'That lawyer that the cops were talking about, was here with Moe many times, I think they often did some business deals, I looked at Monica, 'Let's keep that to ourselves, I don't want to drag Moe's name into the mud.

CHAPTER 9

I was in bed with Monica, when she woke me up and whispered, 'I think there is someone downstairs,' I took my gun from the drawer by my bed and crept downstairs. In the lounge, was a young black guy opening the drawers and cupboards and making a noise.

I knew this guy was no professional, I switched the lights on and pointed my gun, the guy started to put his hands up, then ran, I put the gun down. I had shot enough people, to last me a lifetime, Monica said, 'Who was it.' Shrugging my shoulders, I said,

'Just some amateur burglar, maybe we forgot to lock the door?' But I had seen that guy's face before. I liked Miami, the weather, the laid-back attitude, the plush bars and restaurants

If I moved here, I could still do business, but it would have to be wholesale, I had a good reputation, buy in bulk, then moved it on, to guys who would break it down into individual joints, to sell on the street, it would only be half the profit, but I would never have to see the stuff, a few phone calls, and no risks.

I had to have another honest supplier, I contacted the old guy that I gave a million to invest, we met at the same plush hotel, in the same stateroom, he had one of his sons with him, and he waved me to sit down, he looks at me and said, first of all, you have our sympathy. Moe was my friend also I was told that he left everything to you, he had a one-million-dollar investment with me, it is yours when it is to be paid out, I was shocked, I looked at the old man,

'You could have kept that and said nothing,' he nodded,

I told you, we are honest dealers, and what would you have done if you had found out? 'Now, how can I help you?

With Moe gone, I need an honest supplier, it has to be pure hash' the old man thought for a moment, 'I know a dozen suppliers, but an honest one, that could be a problem! Let me make a couple of calls,' the old man left the room, his son rang for coffee, and we sat in silence, drinking coffee.

The door opened, and the old man sat down with a sheet of paper, I think I have got you a guy who can supply you, but it will be a cash upfront deal, but at the same price that you bought from Moe.

I met the supplier that the old man had recommended, a young Mexican, who looked and dressed like a gangster, he had three Mexican girls with him, we met on a bench at the park, and he shook my hand, Hombre! I am Pedro, I hear that you are a straight-up guy, I usually only deal with my Mexican buddies, I said, how about a Scotsman who drinks tequila? it was meant to be funny, but no one laughed.

We talked business for an hour, then Pedro invited me to a Mexican restaurant, and one of his girls sat next to me, 'My name is Angel, she smiled, short for Angelica,'

I said 'My name is Santa, short for Santa,' she looked puzzled, we got chatting, and she told me that she was a cousin of Pedro and that she did his books.

Angel told me that she was studying to be an accountant in Miami, but that she worked for Pedro, on her time off, I talked with Pedro about going wholesale, and he said, no problem, just tell me when, and we will work something out, with his guys delivering to Los Angeles.

I thought I didn't need the money, I had millions, and maybe it was time to enjoy the cash, but first, a visit to a lawyer's office, the lawyer said, 'OK. what are your instructions.' He called a girl in with a notepad and started writing, I told her, 'One million each to, Carla, Albi, Merri. Monica, and the rest of the money to the nun, with the down and outs on the main street, Los Angeles.' She wrote down all the addresses. As I stepped out to my car, I felt that I had done another good deed, to clear my conscience.

One evening on my way back to the house, I stopped outside a store, to pick up some beers and wine for the house, as I went to pay, a guy standing next to me, pulled out a gun, and the shopkeeper put his hands up, the gunman pointed his gun at me, and growled, and you too buddy.

I put my shopping onto the counter, and put my hands up, the shopkeeper put some money onto the counter, and the guy pointed the gun at me, 'Empty your pockets,' I put my wallet, and some change onto the counter, the gunman said, 'And the watch,' I looked at the guy, and said, 'This is sentimental,' he hit me on the side of the head with the gun, and pulled the watch off my wrist.

The shop keeper, bent down behind the counter, and the gunman, startled, pointed the gun across the counter, I grabbed the gun with one hand and punched his jaw with the other hand, the gunman fell backwards, into a stack of tomato cans, the shopkeeper suddenly had a shotgun in his hands, and fired at the guy struggling to get from under a pile of tomato cans, then ran out the shop door.

I picked up my watch and money, paid for my shopping, and went to my car, I put my groceries in the boot, and then I heard a moan from the front of the car, the gunman was sitting up against the bumper, holding his arm, I helped him into the car, he said, 'Are you taking me to the cops?' I parked at the hospital car park.

At the desk, I told the nurse, that he had been shot by some unknown kid, a nurse, and a doctor, came and put him into a wheelchair, I gave the nurse five hundred dollars, 'Will this cover the bill?' she nodded, give the guy the change,' I went out to my car, feeling good, but the watch wasn't sentimental, it was junk.

I had made my mind up, I was going to move to Miami, I had Moe's beautiful house and millions stashed away, I invited Albi and his skinny wife to come down to Miami, and stay a couple of days, I could explain to him that I was going wholesale and that he could sort out the Los Angeles side. Albi and now his not-so-skinny wife stayed three days at the house.

Monica did the hosting, taking Alibi's wife shopping, and we would take them to some fancy restaurants and show them a good time, Albi and I, worked on a plan to go wholesale, with Albi using some of the hash to make individual joints for our existing customers. Albi had taken his brother-in-law on board to help him.

Can you trust the guy? People get jealous when they see someone else making money, Albi said, he is my brother-in-law! I nodded, just be careful brother, and keep in touch, we can make millions if we are careful, he nodded.

I took Albi and his wife to the airport and said our goodbyes, back at the house Pedro and Angel were sitting by the pool, Monica said that they turned up and made themselves at home with the drinks and food! Pedro and I arranged the first shipment of hash to Los Angeles, I handed over fifteen thousand dollars, Angel counted the money, nodded to Pedro, and then put the cash into her bag.

Monica had been AWOL for two days, and she didn't answer her phone, so I drove over to her house, a little two-storey house with kids' toys in the garden, a young guy in his vest and pants, opened the door with a beer can in his hand and a week's stubble on his chin, what do you want? Monica does some work for me, and she hasn't shown up for a couple of days, is she unwell? He took a swig of beer and then shouted for Monica.

Monica came to the door with a child in her arms and a black eye, the guy pushed her back into the lobby, 'She doesn't work for you anymore, now get off my property before I kick your arse.' I saw Monica shake her head from the lobby, I walked away with the guy still shouting and cursing.

Back at the house, I rang Moe's other girlfriend, Alice, and asked if she could help out with the housekeeping, she arrived in a taxi, with two suitcases, I showed her a room and said are you staying over? She looked surprised, 'I thought I was included in the housekeeping duties,' she smiled, and I smiled.

Alice told me that the arrangement with Moe was that Monica was a housekeeper and Alice would help out and stay with Moe as his girlfriend. Alice smiled, and said, 'Shall we carry on with that arrangement?' Why not! She was beautiful. Alibi's wife rang me and told me that Alibi's brother-in-law had stolen a shipment of hash and had set up in business for himself, she said that Albi was trying to recover the hash and that he wasn't going tell you after you warned him about taking on family, that would be jealous of the money.

I flew up to LAX. Booked into a hotel, rented a car and drove to Albie's house, his wife let me in, and over coffee, she said that Albie had been gone for two days, and he had not rung! She wrote the address for her brother's house, then weeping said, find Albie and bring him home.

I found her brother's house with two guys sitting on the porch drinking beer, I walked up to them and said, any hash for sale, one guy said, you have come to the right place man, show me the money! I took out two, hundred-dollar bills, and the first guy took me into the house and said, 'Sit in the kitchen, I'll be back in a minute,' as soon as he had gone, I started to search the downstairs rooms.

The basement door was locked, and the guy came from upstairs, he looked at me standing by the basement, what are you doing? He came towards me, pulling a knife from his belt, I had my gun in my hand and shot him in the leg, he fell to the floor screaming, and holding his leg. The other guy from the porch ran in, I punched him, and he dropped to the floor. I pointed my gun at the guy still screaming. 'Give me the key to the basement or I'll shoot your other leg,' he shook his head, 'I have not got the key,' I put my gun onto his good leg, 'OK,' he screamed, and pulled a bunch of keys from his pocket, I found the one for the basement and opened the door.

I switched the light on and could smell hash, I went down into the basement, and in the middle of the bundles of hash, was Albie, gagged and tied up hand and foot, I got him up into the kitchen, he sobbed, 'Sorry boss. It was all going well when a little birdie told me that my brother-in-law was my dealing hash on the side, when I asked him about this, one of his gang knocked me out, and that is where you found me, sorry.'

I put my hand on his shoulder, 'Albie, together we will sort this out, but how close is your wife to her brother?' 'She can't stand him and told me that he was not to be trusted,' he looked at me,

'But I knew better.' The guy whom I had knocked out was standing at the kitchen door with a knife, I fired a shot over his head, he dropped the knife and ran outside.

'Where is your brother-in-law now,' Albie wrote an address down and handed it to me, 'He is doing deals for the hash at that place, I'll come with you,' 'No Albie, you go home to your family, he doesn't know me, so he will think that I am just another dealer.'

I parked outside the address that Albie gave me, there were several other cars parked on the driveway, a huge black guy showed me into a room full of guys and gals drinking beer and smoking hash, I was handed a beer, 'Are you here to buy?' I nodded, and a small wiry, well-dressed guy stood on a chair, I could tell this was my guy, he looked like Albie's wife.

He held his hand up and the room quieted down, 'We are here to bid for fifteen thousand dollars' worth of top-quality hash, and you all know if it's cut, it will be more like fifty thousand worth,' there were a lot of nodding heads.

'Who will start the bidding at sixty thousand,' I held my hand up and said, 'One hundred thousand,' everyone in the room turned round in my direction. One guy said, 'I know this guy, he was one of the biggest dealers in Los Angeles,' I pushed through the crowd and pulled the guy off the chair, 'This hash belongs to a guy you all know, Albie, this guy stole Albi's hash.'

The crowd went quiet, one guy said, 'Is the hash for sale or not?' I pulled my gun out and held it against the little guy's head,

'Not! Unless Albie says so.' I then dragged the little guy through the crowd and out to the driveway, I looked at him and said,

'This is my hash, Albie deals with me, if I see your miserable face near my hash again, I'll arrange to have you disappear, and your sister says you are no brother of hers.'

Over the next two days, Albie with the help of a couple of guys moved all the hash back to Albie's warehouse, back at Albies house we discussed getting someone to help Albie that he could trust. I drove downtown to speak to Felipe at his garage. His legs were sticking out from under a car, I grabbed and pulled them, and he looked up, his face covered in oil, 'George,' he stood up and hugged me.

We sat in his little office with a beer, and he told me everything that was happening, he said that Merri had baby number two, and her mother had married off both her sisters, we laughed, and he said, 'Have you found a wife yet?' He smiled and said, 'I know some senoritas that would make good wives,' we both laughed, it was good to see Felipe again.

I went round to my old apartment block and spoke to the same doorman, he was in bad health, I gave him a fifty-dollar note for old times, and he hugged me and wished me good luck, I went into the bar where I first started dealing in the hash, it had changed hands, but I recognized some of the old drunks propping the bar up.

I walked to the street where I first met the nun who dished out the soup and bread to the down and outs, she was still there, and when I walked up to her, she smiled and said, 'Have you found forgiveness yet?' I smiled, 'I am working on its sister,' I handed her five hundred dollars, and she said, 'I'll only accept this if it will ease your conscience,' then laughed, once again she made me feel humbled.

It's a five-hour flight from LA to Miami, plenty of time to think and reflect, I had sorted out Albie's troubles, but it won't be too long before there would be more problems to sort, Albie was loyal and honest, but the job had got too big for him to manage on his own, and with the money that he was making, he had lost his edge and grown soft, he would take his wife and kid for a walk in the park, and eat ice cream, when he should have been sorting out problems.

Back at the house, there were more problems, Monica was back, she had thrown her husband out, and installed her mother to look after her kid, then moved back to my house to find Alice had moved in, the next day sitting at the pool I asked Alice to fetch me a whisky and ice, Monica shouted from the kitchen, 'Got it!'—Help me!

That night I went to my bedroom, and there were Alice and Monica both sitting up in my bed, Alice said, 'Do you prefer one side or the middle, I went to the spare room and locked the door. the drama had begun, I called a meeting in the kitchen over breakfast,

'We will have alternate nights, or both of you sleep in your rooms if you can't agree.' When I thought, I've had worse problems.

Between swimming, playing tennis and two beautiful ladies to serve my every wish, it was a good life, I had joined the local golf club, rubbing shoulders with the movers and shakers, I had a tan, and the gym had worked wonders, but nothing is perfect, I craved adventure, I needed excitement, who wants perfect.

I decided to sell hash in Miami, I didn't need the money, I had millions, I asked around, but it seemed like a closed shop, I couldn't get anyone to tell me what the hash scene was in Miami, then one afternoon I got all the information I needed, I was playing golf with this retired cop, we stopped playing while he lit his pipe.

'I was given a message to pass on to you,' he took a forty-five bullet from his pocket,

'Here, these guys only give one warning, if I were you, I would take the warning,' he puffed on his pipe, I should stop asking around, now let's play golf.'

Back at the clubhouse, over a beer, the cop said, 'I know these guys, they would have you killed over an insult, please, I need a golf partner,' we both laughed.

I decided to forget the idea of selling hash in Miami, I had to think of something else, was I getting soft?

I decided to hire a Mexican gardener, he was a guy that my neighbour used, so with the girls and the gardener, we sat at the pool table with drinks and worked out a plan to reshape the grounds, I told the gardener, 'Pablo, I would like a glasshouse, to warm the young seedlings,' he smiled and said, 'Senor, it's ninety degrees today, we all laughed.'

So, there we were, the girls, Monica and Alice in bikinis, gloves and work boots, and Pablo shaking his head, with me sitting by the pool, under a parasol with a whisky and ice, trying to figure out my next move.

I was invited to a dinner at my posh golf club, Monica was with her mother and kid that night so I took Alice, she had bought a new dress for the Dinner, over a few drinks before dinner, I said, 'Alice, you look gorgeous,\ she kissed me and said, 'Then marry me, I coughed and took a swig of my drink.

'Listen, Alice, I think we are being called to the dining table.'

Alice went to the toilet, and I was aware of a woman hovering at my arm. Turning to face her, I asked, 'Can I help you, love?' She looked like a middle-aged woman, but her eyes told me she was younger, her hair was not dyed, with wisps of grey creeping through, no makeup and a plain dress, 'How can I help?'

She said that her husband was in trouble with the cops, and she was told that I might be able to help. She looked to me like some downtrodden wife, yet here she was seeking help for him,

'I'll have to speak to him,' she went over to a fat, bald well-dressed guy, who came over and said, 'Hi bud,' I am sorry to say, that I took an instant dislike to him, he was well dressed, yet his wife was looking like a down and out.

He said that he was a struck-off lawyer and that the Miami police had it in for him, he said that he was stopped, and charged with driving under the influence, 'So how can I help?' He told me that he had photos from private eyes, of one of the cops that were having an affair with one of the female assistant prosecutors.

What's in it for me? He said, 'What do you want?'

'I may want a favour in the future,' he nodded.

'And something else, take your wife to a beauty shop, and buy her some new clothes, deal?' he nodded again.

'OK, get me the photos and I'll see what I can do!' Alice came back, she was a little drunk. At the table she was a little flirty with the waiter, she smiled, 'I bet he would like to marry me.' She showed me a little slip of paper, Alice smiled and said, 'Look, he has given me his phone number, see, some guys do fancy me,'

Back at the house, it was dusk and still warm, I had a drink on the patio then stripped off and dived into the pool, Alice dived into the pool behind me, hugged me and said, 'That waiter didn't give me his number, I made it up to make you jealous,' I kissed her nose, and said, 'Well, you did make me jealous, I lied! but it made her happy.'

CHAPTER 10

I went to the main police headquarters, and at the desk, I asked for Officer Dean, the desk sergeant said,

'Why do you want to speak to Dean? I said a personal matter.

'He is off duty and probably at home, here is his phone number, thanks, I walked out of the building and went to a phone booth.

A guy answered.

'Yes, Harry Dean speaking, and who are you?' I said that I had a delicate matter to talk to about. there was a moment of silence, 'OK, meet me in twenty minutes. He gave me the address of a pub,

I ordered a beer and sat in a booth, a big heavy guy came in, looked around the pub and nodded to me, I nodded back, and he sat down with a beer and said, 'What's this all about?'

I put the photo on the table, and he smiled, 'I know who has put you up to this, that son of a bitch, dishonest ex-lawyer, what does he want, to get me fired?' I said, 'I don't like the guy either, but nobody is going to get fired, all I need you to do is misplace the court papers on his drunk driving case,' The cop looked at me and shook his head, 'Do you think that will be the end of it? This guy will hold this photo over our heads till next time.' I began to feel sorry for him.

'Look, take care of this matter and I will get copies of the photos,' he smiled, 'Why would you do that?' I said, 'Because the guy is a fraud,' The cop finished his beer.

'OK, I'll see what I can do.'

'Listen, I said, I need to get the guy out of his house for a couple of hours, can you do that?' He nodded,

'How about this evening around seven,' he smiled, 'I can arrange to have him taken to police headquarters for a couple of hours,

but he is pretty savvy, it will be two hours maximum.'

I sat in my car at the top of the street, as a cop car pulled up outside the guy's house, and watched as he was led out in handcuffs, I pulled opposite the driveway, got my bag of tricks and went to the back door.

Inside the house I found an office, the door was locked, and it took me five minutes to get in, he had steel cabinets all around the walls, and some were unlocked, I skipped those and started to force the other ones. Inside one of the drawers was a small safe, it took me almost twenty minutes to get it open.

Bingo, there was a folder with a dozen photos, some of the cop with the woman, and the others of two guys lying naked on a bed. I checked his camera, empty, then I took the motherboard out of his computer. As I put it into my bag, I heard the front door being opened, I fled out the back door and round to my car and took off.

I met the cop at the same pub. We sat down with a beer, and he handed me a file with the charges of the lawyer's case, he smiled, things get lost all the time in the office. I handed him the file with the photos of him and the prosecutor, he looked at the photos in the file, nodded, and said, 'Thanks, I owe you a favour.'

We clinked glasses and took a drink, I put my glass down.

'By the way, there were CTC cameras at his house, he may have me charged with burglary. The cop put his beer down,

'If he does, well, you know how things get mislaid at headquarters,' we shook hands and he waved goodbye.

I had just finished a round of golf with Stan, my retired cop golfing partner, I went to the plush bar area for a drink, while Stan went out to meet his daughter, a waiter came up to me and said, 'There is a young lady would like to speak to you, he pointed over to a seating area by the windows. I took my drink over to the table, the woman was about thirty, good-looking and well-dressed, I sat down and said, 'You wanted to talk to me?'

'Yes, I have been told that you took care of a matter that could have caused me some embarrassment,' she lowered her eyes,

'Thank you, is there any way that I can return the favour?' I thought for a moment.

'Well yes, I may be charged with burglary shortly, she took a sip of her drink, 'Yes, I have been told of that possibility, you will know of course that the person who will bring that charge is the same person that was blackmailing me and my friend,' she smiled,

'I am the assistant prosecutor. That case will not see daylight. Now if you will excuse me, my husband is joining me soon,' she shook my hand. 'If there is anything that I can help you with in the future, please ask.'

As went back to the bar, I felt a tap on my shoulder, it was Charlie, the bald, well-dressed ex-lawyer, he growled at me,

'You bastard, you broke into my office and stole the photos, now I have no protection against that cop and his girlfriend, that bitch will come after me,' I looked at him, 'The drink-driving case has disappeared as I agreed,' he smiled and nodded. 'Now you do what we agreed,' he looked puzzled, 'What was that?

'That you would treat your wife to a beauty shop and a new wardrobe.' He stepped back and gave a little laugh.

'Forget that, nobody tells me how to treat that woman!' He laughed and walked away, I followed him out to the car park. He wound his car window down and said, 'I am the king of my castle.' I punched him hard, his nose spurted blood, and then I walked back to the bar and ordered a large whisky. Ten minutes later, two cops came up to me at the bar, 'Put your hands behind you, sir.

They put the handcuffs on tight, then he read me my rights, the cop said, 'We are going to take you downtown and book you for assault.

A waiter came up to the cop and whispered in his ear. They both went over to a couple sitting at a table by the windows. I watched them in conversation with the assistant prosecutor.

The cops came back and took the cuffs off, then without another word, left the club. Back at the house, the girls and Pedro were busy planting all the new shrubs that had been delivered, the garden had started to take shape, and I sat on the patio with a drink, watching the girls in their bikinis and work boots helping poor Pedro.

The phone rang, it was Albie's wife, he had been arrested, she was crying, she told me where he was being held. I rang a young lawyer that I had used before, he was a hotshot and had just been promoted. I told him to get Albie bailed out and report back, three hours later he rang and said that Albie was free and that the charge was supplying hash, one of the dealers had made a deal with a cop, to shop Albie for a lesser charge on the dealer, he had been caught in a sting.

The lawyer said that the charge would get Albie a year in jail, or he would arrange a bribe of five thousand dollars to get the charge reduced to a minor offence with a fine of a thousand dollars, I told him to pay the bribe and the fine. I rang Albie and arranged for him to pay the lawyer that same day.

Albie had been sending me parcels of cash every month regularly, he was an honest guy, but I felt that the business was a little too much for one guy to handle, there were wolves back in Los Angeles, who would gobble him up if they knew that we didn't have the protection that I said we had.

I rang Andy, the student from San Francisco, and he told me he had passed his law bar exams, and now he was a fully qualified lawyer, but he found it hard to get a position in a law firm, and said, it was him selling hash that kept him afloat. I put a proposition to him if he helps Albie to run the hash-selling side of the business, I'll set him up in his own office, and he agreed straight away.

I flew up to Los Angeles and met Albie and Andy at my hotel bar, we all had a drink, sat at a table and worked out a plan, with Albie selling the hash fifty per cent joints and fifty per cent wholesale, and Andy overseeing the whole business, in return, I would set Andy up in his own office in Los Angeles, and he could still deal with his contacts in San Francisco.

I gave Andy a couple of phone numbers of tough guys, that, for a fee would take care of troublemakers.

I stayed for a week in Los Angeles, setting up an office with Andy, buying office furniture and hiring decorators, Andy introduced me to his girlfriend, Sally, who was going to run his office, Sally was the daughter of a police captain, these were the people who were going to help shift my hash, who'd believe this!

I got a call from the investors to come to the hotel at noon, two days from today, I said my goodbyes and caught the flight to sunny Miami. Monica picked me up at the airport and drove me to the Hotel. parked up, and went shopping with a promise to be back in an hour. I sat at the table with the old guy and his two sons, we all shook hands, and then the old guy put a case onto the table and pushed it to me.

'Here is Moe's investment, one million dollars, returned as one million three hundred thousand, and your investment will be the same, the investment did better than ten per cent.'

Monica was waiting in the Cadillac smoking. We drove to a smart beachfront restaurant. Sitting at a table, overlooking the beach with a million three hundred thousand dollars at my feet, life felt good. After lunch, I took Monica shopping for some clothes, she did not stop smiling the whole afternoon. On the way back to the car I saw Charlie, the bald ex-lawyer with a red-headed girl on his arm.

I gave Monica the bags to put in the car. The lawyer left the girl standing outside a cigar shop, while he went in. I quickly walked up to the girl, 'Excuse me, but I am Doctor Evans. A venereal disease professor, would you tell your husband that I can't see him at my clinic next week, I'll reappoint, thank you.' I walked quickly back to the car with a grin. When we got back to the house, Alice was sitting on the patio. When she saw Monica with the clothes bags, she said, 'Where are my new clothes?' Monica gave Alice a catty smile as she took the bags upstairs, more drama, I kissed Alice,

'It's your turn tomorrow to shop, Alice said, 'I will be up at dawn, what time do the shops open?'

Alice got eight hundred dollars to shop, while I went to the golf club and met my golfing buddy. After a round, we stood at the bar chatting, when Stan, the retired cop said look, 'There are the guys you don't want to mess with.' I looked over to where he nodded and there was the old guy with his two sons, the guys who had given me Moe's invested money the day before, they saw me and nodded, and the cop said, 'You know these guys? Just what kind of business are you in?'

I decided that Miami was to be my home, it had everything that I could ask for, so I was going to fly to Zurich, empty my bank account then invest the money in Miami. I told the girls that I was going off on business, I had done this before, so they just nodded. Alice drove me to the airport and kissed me goodbye. I had a drink at the bar when I recognized a girl standing by herself, it was the girl that I saw with Charlie, the bent lawyer in Miami.

I tapped her on the shoulder, and she turned around and said,

'Hello doctor Evans,' she smiled, 'You are not a doctor,' she shook my hand and said, 'I am Gina, Charlie told me that you were a drug dealer and a rat, but I know that you were trying to warn me, Charlie said that you assaulted him, but that he had beat you up, she smiled again, 'I don't think Charlie could beat up a milk pudding,' we both laughed. Sitting at the bar with a drink, we got talking about Charlie.

She was a short plump girl with a beautiful round face, full lips and long red hair, when she smiled her face lit up. I asked,

'What are you doing here?' She said, 'I am flying to Zurich.'

'What! And so am I, have you booked a hotel there?'

she took a paper from her bag and said, 'It's the Regent Hotel, by the lake,' I slapped my forehead, 'Amazing, that's my hotel also.'

she looked at me, grinned and said, 'Really.'

The plane was half empty, so we sat next to each other.

Over a few drinks, she told me that she frequently made the flight to Zurich to deposit items into safety deposit boxes for clients of Charlie. So that's how he made his money! The fat bastard was hiding money for the gambling casinos and Mafia types in Miami.

CHAPTER 11

We arrived at Zurich airport and took a taxi to the plush Regent Hotel. Gina booked in and said, 'See you later maybe!' I went up to the reception desk, and a young pale-faced guy said, 'Have you a booking sir?' I smiled, 'No, I was hoping that you would have a room for me,' he studied the screen.

'Sorry sir, we are completely booked up for the next two weeks.' I put a hundred-dollar bill on the desk in front of him, and said, 'Perhaps you could check again?' He picked up the money with expertise, that told me he had done this before. He stared at the screen for a moment, then tapped on the keyboard,

'Ah, a bit of luck sir, there has just been a cancellation.'

The room had a balcony that overlooked the lake, I showered and changed, sprayed myself with Joop, and then rang down to reception, asking for the room number for Gina. Her room was only three rooms away on the same floor! I knocked, and Gina opened the door with wet hair and a white bath towel around her. I pushed past her and closed the door, then put my arms around her waist, and kissed her, she smiled, 'You don't waste time,' then kissed me back and let her towel fall to the floor.

When I awoke, it was dark outside, Gina was already showered and dressed. She smiled and said, 'I am taking you to my favourite Italian Restaurant.' Quickly dressed we took a taxi to the centre of town, filled with bars, coffee shops and Restaurants. We sat talking and drinking wine. 'In case you were wondering,' She said, 'It was only a business agreement with Charlie, he tried it on a couple of times, but I found him a creepy type of guy. 'Gina said, 'I met his wife a couple of times, I felt sorry for her,'

I looked up and said, 'I had the feeling that she was content with being the downtrodden wife.'

We finished the meal and left the Restaurant.

Gina knew her way around the town,

'Fancy a drink at a club?' She asked. I kissed her nose,

'Lead on my lovely, I am in your hands,' At the club, Gina knew a few people, mostly Americans, I said, 'Why are they all here?' She smiled, 'They are all wanted men, Mafia types. If they go back to the States, they will do jail time, and this is a nice place to be in exile.'

Back at the hotel, we went to the bar for a nightcap, Gina said 'Tomorrow, I have to conclude my business at the bank and go back to Miami. What are you doing tomorrow?'

'I am doing the same thing, but we don't have to rush back, do we?' She smiled, and said, 'I can show you around this beautiful city,' I nodded.

We finished the drinks and went up in the lift.

As we stepped out Gina kissed me and said, 'Your room or mine?'

The next morning, we shared the shower, then went down for breakfast, I was carrying a large empty bag. Gina had a travel bag with a tin box inside. We called a taxi and then set off to Town. I dropped Gina at a bank on the outskirts of the city and arranged to meet at a coffee house in town, then went to my bank.

The manager greeted me with a small glass of whisky.

The bank staff was celebrating an employee getting a promotion as a manager to another branch. I told the manager that I wanted to empty my account, and he said, 'Do you mean that we won't see you again?' I smiled and said, 'Never say never.

We went down to the security box room. He opened a panel and took out a large metal box.

I gave my signature and then pressed the digits, the manager stepped out of the room, and I opened the box, it was packed with high-denomination dollar bills.

I stuffed the money into my large bag, the cash was taped up in ten-thousand-dollar bundles.

I forgot just how much money I had put into this bank.

I said my goodbyes to the manager with a gift of five hundred dollars, which he quickly put into his pocket, then whispered,

'There is no need sir, but should you need any help in the future.' He gave me a card with his number. We shook hands and left.

Gina was sitting at a table outside the coffee house, she had ordered me a whisky with ice, over the drink she said that she thought that she had been followed from the bank. She pointed to a dark sedan sitting down the street, I was nervous, I had not told Gina that I had over a million dollars in a bag sitting under the table. I finished my whisky and got a taxi back to the hotel.

I put the money into the hotel safe and then met Gina at the bar. I looked around the bar area and saw the same guy that had stolen Carla's bag from the hotel bar, with a couple of guys. These were the guys that had followed Gina from the bank. They thought that she had taken money out, instead of putting money in.

I went to the reception desk and bought a bag, then stuffed it with local newspapers from the news desk. Zipped it up and returned to the bar. The three guys were now standing at the bar. I told Gina to visit the toilet, and then moments later I followed. Hiding behind a pillar. I watched them pick up the bag, one guy put it under his coat, and then they all quickly left. I would have loved to see their faces when they opened the bag, he would have realized that I had seen him again.

Gina was a tiger in bed, that red hair should have given me a clue. As I drifted into sleep, Gina would nudge me and kiss my ear,

'Wake up, time for round two.' Over breakfast, I said to Gina, 'Why don't Charlie's clients invest money in Miami, she smiled, 'The investors won't touch them, it's dirty money from arms deals, insurance frauds, scams and other stuff that the investors won't touch.' Gina said, 'Are you married? Or maybe a steady girlfriend? I smiled, 'I have two girlfriends, I explained the setup at the house, and Gina smiled and said, 'Any room for another?'

I nodded, 'I could maybe have a sleeping partner.'
She leaned over the table and kissed my cheek,

'I'd settle for that...for now. We flew back to Miami, and at the airport bar, I rang Monica to come and pick me up. I said to Gina, 'Are you getting picked up or do you want a lift? She smiled,

'I'll take a lift. I want to meet the competition.'
As the Cadillac pulled up, Monica leaned out of the window.

'I missed you.' She looked at Gina, then pulled a face.

'And where would *you* like to be dropped off?' Nobody said a word on the journey to Miami. There was a chill in the air, even though it was Forty-five outside!

We dropped Gina at her apartment and then drove home. Sitting outside on the patio with a drink, Alice was in the pool and Monica and I were chatting at the table. She stared and spat out, 'Who was she?' I pretended I didn't know who she meant. 'Whom do you mean my love?' Monica glared.

'That red-headed bitch, is she your comfort girl when you are abroad?' I forced a laugh, stood and dived into the pool.

I went to dinner at the golf club with Alice and Monica. We were chatting to other golfers that I had gotten to know when the assistant prosecutor came over and started talking to me,

'I see you have your hareem with you tonight,' I said, 'No, those are my gardeners,' we both laughed, she said, 'I wonder if you can help a friend of mine, he is a lawyer, who sometimes helps me with some difficult specialist cases.'

'Sure, if you think I can help!' She said as she walked away,

'I will send him over when he arrives.'

Alice got a little drunk as usual, so Monica took her home, before she did her party trick, by taking her clothes off. I stood at the bar, speaking to Stan, my golfing buddy, when a guy said, 'Can I buy you guys a drink,' I turned around and there was the guy in the photo, lying on the bed with another guy, Stan said, 'No thanks, I have to go to my wife and daughter at the table.'

The guy seemed nervous and constantly looked around. He whispered, 'Where can we talk? We stepped outside onto the huge patio.

It was lit up with string lights, hanging from the trees and fences.

'I don't know how to say this, but I am being blackmailed, over a foolish thing that I did years ago,' he turned his head away. I smiled and asked, 'Was this blackmailer holding an incriminating photo of you with a friend,' he lowered his head and nodded.

He looked with tears in his eyes, I put my hand on his shoulder, 'If I can sort this matter out, what's in it for me,' he put his head down, and lowered his voice, 'How much do you want?'

'Nothing my friend, but I may ask you for a favour one day,' he looked puzzled when I repeated, 'Yes, nothing but a favour.'

We arranged to meet at a coffee house on the beachfront. Alice and Monica came with me. I gave them some money to shop and after a few moments, I saw a guy in a cap and huge sunglasses, peering behind a tree, Like some kind of Inspector Clouse au.

I waved him over and told him to sit down, and got him a coffee, he seemed to be more nervous than ever. I said, 'Relax and drink your coffee,' he took a sip and then pushed a paper bag across the table, he whispered behind his coffee cup, 'There are five thousand dollars in the bag, I will get you some more by the weekend,' I pushed the bag back, 'I told you, I don't want your money, I said if you just do me a favour in the future.' I took out an envelope and passed it across the table. He took the photo out looked for a second and said, 'Are there any copies?' My eyes widened.

'What do I need copies for?' he finished his coffee staring at the table in silence then stood and went without saying a word.

The girls came back in a taxi with bags and parcels, Alice said, 'Sorry, no change,' they both laughed.

We drove out of town to a little village by the seaside and found a nice-looking bar. Out on the patio, the girls were chatting away about the clothes that they had bought. I was looking out to sea, when I noticed a guy waving his arms, then disappearing.

He was drowning! I ran across the beach, dived into the water and started swimming as hard as I could.

I grabbed the guy and started to pull him back, he was struggling and yelling, 'What are you doing man!' Pointing to a boat fifty yards away with two guys and a cameraman—they were shooting a film!

I got back to the patio, wet through, the girls were laughing when a film guy came over and said, 'Sorry man, we should have warned the people on the beach,' he looked at Alice and said, 'Like to earn a hundred bucks for twenty minutes of work,' Alice stood up,

'Will I be in the film.' The film guy nodded and winked at me.

'You'll be famous.'

She went off along the beach with the film guy, Monica and I had a salad and a couple of drinks. Monica muttered, 'She thinks she's a bloody film star. More like a porn star.' Then burst into laughter. Alice came back with a huge grin and said that the director told her that she was a natural, she opened her hand and showed us a hundred bucks. We finished our drinks, drove back to the house and sat around the patio table.

Monica told me that she was a hairdresser before she got married and that she missed the company of the other girls at the salon, she said, 'Do you mind if I do a part-time job at a friend's salon?'

78

Alice and I picked up Monica from the hairdressing salon one afternoon, Monica introduced me to the girl who owned the place, and she told me that it was hard work with three kids, and her husband was abroad for months at a time, she was thinking of selling. She showed me around the salon and said that she owned it outright.

I spoke with Monica about the salon. She said it was hard work, but she loved it. The girl told me that she wanted one hundred thousand dollars for the salon and all the equipment, I rang a surveyor that I had met at the golf club and asked him to look over the salon and tell me what it was worth. In the meantime, the cash was building up from the hash business in Los Angeles.

The large metal cupboard in my garage was nearly full of parcels of money. I spoke on the phone with Andy, and apart from some guys given the dealer's hassle, all's well. Andy said that he was getting clients on the legal side.

The investor's son rang me, my investment had paid out and would be at the hotel to pick it up now. Alice dropped me at the hotel, then went off shopping, the old guy was sitting at the table with a large bag in front of him, he grinned as he pushed the bag towards me, and said, 'Not a bad return for your money.' I told the old guy that I had up to three million to invest if the return was worth it. The old guy's eyes lit up, he pointed a finger at me,

'There will be a call for a huge investment in a couple of weeks, I'll let you know when the call comes in.'

The bag with the money filled up the metal cupboard, the next parcel of cash would have to go under the bed.

The Mexican hash supplier, Pedro, said that he was coming to Miami to see me and discuss a price adjustment, I didn't like the sound of that, was he getting greedy? Or were all the commodity prices going up?

I was standing at the golf club bar when there was a tap on my shoulder. I turned to see Gina, 'How are you my lovely?' She had her hair up in a huge bun and wore a short flowery skirt, that showed off her legs. She smiled, showing her perfect white teeth.

'I am here with Charlie, he wants to talk with you,' she winked, and by the way, he doesn't know that we know each other.

I sat down with my drink opposite Charlie, he was wearing a Hawaiian shirt which made him look even fatter, he smiled, 'Thanks for coming over, I know that we have had our issues in the past, but I want to discuss a business deal that you might be interested in.' He turned to me and said, 'Where are my manners, this is Gina,' we shook hands. She smiled, and you are Santa?

Charlie said, 'Gina, go fetch us some drinks from the bar,'

We chatted till Gina came back with the drinks, a gin and tonic for Charlie, an orange juice for Gina and a whisky with ice for me. Charlie picked up his drink, then paused and said, 'How did you know what Santa wanted to drink?' Gina smiled, 'I guessed, he looked like a whisky guy to me,' Charlie nodded and drank his gin.

'So, Charlie, what the deal you wanted to talk about,' He said,

'I have clients who wanted to invest some large sums in Miami,

and the word on the street was that you were an honest John with contacts.' I remember Gina telling me when we were in Zurich that the investors in Miami would not touch the dirty money that these guys were trying to invest.

Now Charlie was trying to con me into getting me to put their money into the investors that I knew and pass it off as mine. I said nothing about what I knew.

'What amounts are we talking about?' Charlie's eyes lit up,

'Up to twenty million for a start. There will be plenty for you and me in the deal, what do you say?' I paused then asked, 'Charlie, who are these money men?' He grinned; 'You shouldn't know, and does it matter?'

'Let me think it over Charlie,' he looked with a serious face, 'Don't take too long Santa, or I may give someone else the offer,' Gina smiled, Charlie got up from the table and said to Gina,

'Come to my office tomorrow, I have an errand that I want you for, and bring your passport, Gina nodded. Charlie shook my hand.

After Charlie left, Gina said, 'What shall we do now?' We sat at the bar, Gina said, 'Charlie wants me to take money to Zurich tomorrow, why don't you come with me, she smiled, remember the Regent Hotel?' We both laughed. I leaned over and kissed her and said, 'Maybe next time if you give me a little notice.' Gina waved her finger, 'I will hold you to that.'

CHAPTER 12

Back at the house, Monica said that the surveyor wants to speak to you about the hairdressing salon, and some guy called Charlie said to tell you that the clock is ticking. Was the guy joking, I only spoke to him a couple of hours ago. I rang the surveyor, and he gave me a breakdown, it was only a few repairs that were needed, he also looked at the books, and thought they had been doctored, but the building and the equipment were worth the price, regardless of the books. Taking Monica to the meeting.

I made the offer, and the salon girl started crying, and said,

'I will go to the lawyers tomorrow and get the papers ready for you to sign, I said, 'Thank you, but there is one other condition,' She went silent for a moment.

'That you stay for a week to help Monica ease into the running of the business,' She laughed, 'I was going to do that anyway, I like Monica, I wasn't going to grab the money and run.' We both laughed. Monica said, 'Speak to you tomorrow.'

I was glad to get rid of some of the money from the steel cupboard and do something that would do good for Monica.

The next day I stuffed one hundred thousand dollars into a bag, then met the salon lady at the lawyer's office, I signed the papers and put the bag of money onto his desk. He called in an office girl to count the cash.

The lawyer said it is most unusual to get cash. I suspected he thought it was money laundering. One hour later the deal was done, Monica hugged and kissed me, she smiled and said, 'How can I thank you, I put my finger on my cheek. I'll have to think of something. *She had already "thanked" me that morning.* Then we all went to the nearest pub to celebrate.

I didn't see much of Monica over the next month, but Alice and I would look into her salon when we were in town shopping, she now had four girls working at the salon, and business was booming.

One afternoon Alice and I were having a coffee with Monica in the salon when two guys walked in, Monica got up from the table,

'Sorry guys, it's a women's only salon,' the guys came over to our table, one was a tall thin guy with a beard, and the other one was short with a red face and a bald head, the thin guy grinned,

'We aren't here for a haircut, we are here to tell you that if you want to stay in business, it'll be one hundred bucks every week,' the bald guy laughed, 'And we don't give credit,' they high-fived each other. I said, 'And what happens if we don't want to pay, the tall one leaned over and grabbed my shirt collar, as he did, I punched him in the mouth, and he fell on the floor with his hand on his mouth trying to stem the blood. I grabbed the bald guy as he started to run, and sat him down at the table, he looked at me and growled, 'You don't know who you are dealing with buddy.'

The thin guy stood still holding his mouth, I smiled and said,

'I have a lot of contacts in this town, so if you want a war, I'll make sure that you two bums are the first casualties.'

They walked out muttering and swearing.

Monica had security cameras in the salon, so I got a clear copy of the two guys entering the salon, Monica was shaken,

'What if they came back? I took Alice to the police headquarters to speak to my cop friend. He showed us into his office,

'What can I do for you?' I told him what had happened at the salon, and showed him the pictures of the two guys, he looked at the pictures for a moment then said, 'The short fat one is out on bail, the other guy is on probation,' we all laughed. He wrote down an address and said, 'Here this is where you will find them.'

I took Alice back to the house and then drove to the address on the note, it was a bar in a rough part of town, I walked in and saw the two of them sitting at a table, I sat down and said,

'Listen, guys, I know that life can be tough, but I know that if that salon owner makes a complaint to the cops, it'll be back to jail for you guys, but I have persuaded her not to press charges.'

I took two fifty-dollar notes and put them on the table,

'Stay away from the salon, they both nodded. the little bald guy shook my hand and said, 'Thanks, buddy,' I walked out of the bar, feeling like a boy scout who had just done a good deed. Charlie rang me, 'Look, do you want to invest the money for my clients, or are you going to pass up this opportunity to make thousands in commission? Well.' I said. 'Sorry

Charlie, but I am up to my neck in deals to take on anymore,' Charlie started swearing,

'You'll regret this you punk,' the phone went dead.

Ten minutes later Gina rang me, she was laughing,

'You have pissed off Charlie, I am in his office, and he has thrown half the office at the wall, then he charged out, and he said to me, what am I going to tell my clients, I thought I had that sucker in the palm of my hand.' Gina said, 'So now you owe me a favour, how about taking me out to a fancy restaurant, then to a hotel for a nightcap, just like the Regent Hotel in Zurich?' She laughed, I thought for a moment and said, 'Here is the deal Gina, next time you go to Zurich, I'll go with you, and we will have a romantic couple of days, and I'll take you shopping, just give me a couple of days' notice.'

At the house I had a visitor, it was Monica's husband, we shook hands, and Alice brought us coffee and sat with us, he said,

'I would like to get back with Monica so that I can see my kid, and I miss Monica,' Alice lifted her voice and said, 'Are you sure it is not because Monica is a success and making big bucks?' He smiled, and Alice nodded.

'I'll speak to Monica. But no promises, you were a lousy husband.

She went off into the lounge and picked up the phone. I sat chatting with the guy when Alice came back and sat down. 'Monica said that she never stopped you from seeing the kid,

It was you who never came to see him, and she doesn't want you to come near her,

he stood and shouted, 'Bitch, I am her husband, so half of that salon is mine, and she can support me, I am going for custody as well.' Alice said, 'Sit down, and we will tell you some facts, first of all, Monica does not own the salon, she has a lease with the owner of the salon, and you would never get custody as an absent father,' he smiled, 'I have been told that she will have to pay me something,' I said, 'Who told you that?' He stood and stared at Alice,

'A lawyer called Charlie, he said that he would act for me pro bono, I guess that means for no fee, so the bitch has to make me an offer.' I smiled, 'Listen, my friend, Charlie is a struck-off lawyer, he is not allowed to practice in this state.

look, what amount of cash are you looking for to disappear from Monica's life,' rubbing his hands, his face lit up,

'Make me an offer, and make it worth my while.'

'OK, fifty thousand, he laughed.

'Sorry pal, I was thinking more like half a million, at least. I looked at the guy grinning and said, 'Wait here,' I went into the lounge and rang Charlie,

'I have a client of yours here at my house, asking for a half-million bucks to leave a friend of mine alone.' Charlie said, 'Yes, I represent him, sorry, but business is business, we will settle for a half million, and sign the divorce papers.' I slammed the phone down. I went back and told the guy, we will be in touch

I drove down to Monica's salon, we all sat down, and I explained what had gone on.

'George, he is only back because he was told about the salon, all he wants is money, but I won't give the bum a cent. I want a divorce, and besides, I have a new boyfriend, she smiled, but if you ever need company,' she winked. The conversation drifted.

'When am I going to meet this boyfriend,' Monica said,

'How about Saturday night, we planned a meeting and left.

Back at the house, Alice had just signed for a parcel.

It was money from Los Angeles. The safe was almost full again.

I rang the old guy whom I had invested with before, and he said that he had a small developer who was looking for three million at ten per cent, we agreed to meet and give him the money.

The next day I put three million from the safe into a bag, and then with Alice, drove to the hotel and met with the old guy and his two sons, we had a coffee and then got down to business.

'Can you trust this developer?' He nodded, and the old guy smiled 'I have done business with this guy for many years, and he has never let me down.' I handed over the bag with the three million, we all shook hands and I left.

Saturday night, we got dressed up to the nines, Alice looked beautiful in a new dress, and she put on the diamond necklace that I had given her for her birthday. Alice was a stunner, her only problem was she liked to get drunk, then she would do a striptease and sing. She had a beautiful body but a terrible singing voice!

We walked into the restaurant and sat down with Monica and her new boyfriend, Hendry. We chatted. He told me that he was a doctor at the local hospital and that he was training to be a surgeon. We all got a little tipsy, left the restaurant and went to a club, the girls went to the toilet for a chat and fixed their makeup. Hendry said, 'I have to make a few calls.'

I watched him heading for the toilet. I finished my drink and then went to the toilet, as I entered, Hendry and another guy were snorting coke off the table, Hendry waved me over,

'Help yourself, man.' Then carried on snorting it up his nose.

We said our goodbyes, and Hendry whispered 'The coke thing, let's keep it our secret.' Back at the house, I stripped off and took a swim, Alice did the same, I told Alice about seeing Hendry sniffing coke, and she gasped and said,

'If Monica knew she would dump him, she hates druggies,

what are you going to do?' 'I'll do a little checking.

I can't believe that a guy in his position is a cokehead.'

I went to the hospital enquiry desk, and a young black girl with a huge afro said, 'Can I help you sir? I looked over her shoulder at a list of staff. 'I am looking for a doctor who is a member of staff here. She looked at the screen.

'What's his name?' I realized that I only knew his first name. 'His first name is Hendry.' She tapped on the keyboard, then said, 'There is no doctor in this hospital with that first name, I asked, 'Try the surgeons, he told me he was training to be a surgeon.'

The girl tapped on the keyboard.

'No, there are only three surgeons at this hospital, none called Hendry.' She tapped on the keyboard, looked up and said, 'Wait, there is one guy called Hendry in this building, and that is Hendry,

the store's guy, he is in charge of the ins and outs of the hospital materials storeroom, you can find him in the basement. She turned and looked at the wall clock. He is on duty in an hour if you want to speak to him.' I thanked her and told her that she had the best Afro. that I had ever seen.

I rang Monica and asked her out for lunch, we drove to the hospital, and Monica said, 'Where are you taking me? I smiled,

'To see somebody, you know before we had lunch.' We took the lift down to the basement; found the materials room and went in. The room was full of shelves. We rang the bell, and Hendry came through a door, he had a look of shock, Monica said, 'Hendry what are you doing in the basement? Hendry swung a punch at me, and growled, 'Son of a bitch,' he turned around and went back through the door and slammed it shut. Monica laughed,

'So much for Doctor Hendry, what a con artist,' we both laughed over lunch, I looked at Monica and said, 'I wasn't going to let some con artist mess with my Beautiful Monica, no siree.' She said,

'That was something I noticed, how come a doctor had dirty nails,' she laughed. Monica said, 'I miss staying at the house, can I come round and stay this weekend?'

We had lunch then I drove Monica back to the salon, she waved,

'See you at the weekend.' I got a call from Charlie; 'My client has instructed me to tell you that he will sign the divorce papers

for a consideration of ten thousand dollars

and seek no further financial settlement.'

I thought for a moment,

'Put all that in writing, and send it to me and we will consider the offer.' the papers came with the post the next day, and I took them to the lawyer friend of the assistant prosecutor. He shook my hand and sat me down in his huge office. He studied the documents for ages, and kept glancing up at me then said, 'They all seemed in order, but what about custody? If he was to get custody of the kids, he could ask for support. He could come back to court to try and get alimony, but the fact that he got a sum of money and signed a paper agreeing not to make a claim, I don't think that the court would have much sympathy for him.'

I arranged for him to oversee the transaction, I would give the Lawyer the ten thousand dollars and he would give Charlie a cheque.

Monica said thanks when I said that I would pay them ten thousand bucks to get the divorce papers signed.

We all met at the lawyer's office;

Monica didn't make eye contact with her husband. The papers were signed by all parties concerned, with the cheque handed over. Charlie and Monica's husband left, and the lawyer shook my hand,

'How much do I owe you, he shook his head and stared at the floor,'

'You don't owe me anything.

Monica sat next to me on the drive back to the salon,

'I am glad that it's over, and I have a new friend, can I take him to the house this weekend?' life was getting predictable. On Saturday morning Monica arrived with her new boyfriend, John, and we all sat on the patio by the pool talking, I said to Monica,

'I hope John isn't another doctor.' we both laughed.

We ate lunch then drank and played cards till the afternoon,

Alice went to the pool, stripped naked and dived in, Monica said to her boyfriend, 'You will have to forgive her she is a wild child,' then Monica stripped and dived in. Her boyfriend and I followed—but kept our pants on. Wrapped in towels, we sat in the lounge, watching TV. And playing cards, Monica's boyfriend told me that he was in the car importing business. He explained that he arranged for cars to be brought from Mexico into the States then he would sell them to car dealers and garages. He said that car manufacturers would ship new, unsold cars to Mexico, then he would bring them back second-hand, and be excused the tax. He also got a huge discount as the manufacturers needed a cash flow. He'd borrow money from investors at top rates to buy the cars as there was no credit given.

I asked who his investors were, and he smiled, I don't know if I can tell you that information, all I can tell you is that it's an old guy and his two sons who always come up with the money when I need it,

I laughed, that was where my money was going. I said, 'Suppose that I can get you the funds for a lot less a rate than you are paying now. How much do you need.' Looking at me he said,

'Are you serious? Well, I need half a million next week. I shook his hand grinned and said, 'OK, if you check out, I'll get you the money, at eight per cent' he shook my hand again.

'I look forward to doing business with you.' he gave me his name, and company address to check him out.

In the morning John and I sat talking by the pool with coffee, while the girls made breakfast, Monica told me that she had been to his car sales business and that it all looked kosher. I asked my cop friend to check him out, ditto with the lawyer. Everything came back positive; this guy was too good to be true.

A private eye owed me a favour, so I asked him to check John out. I put a half-million dollars into a bag and met with John at Monica's salon. We sat in the back room, surrounded by shampoo boxes. I gave John the bag with the half-million, he said,

'How do you know that I won't run off with the money?

I looked him in the eye and lowered my voice.

'Because I would spend another half-million to arrange your disappearance.' He shook my hand and said, 'If all goes to plan you should have your money plus, back in a couple of months.' He invited us all to come and visit his car sales business at the weekend. He looked at me when he said,

'Just to convince you that I am not some kind of a scam artist.'

Monica followed me into the kitchen to fetch coffee and said, 'Well, what do you think of John? I smiled and said, 'He seems like a good sort, but time will tell my lovely.

The private eye came to the house, I sat him down, and Alice brought us coffee, he looked at Alice and said, 'Got anything a little stronger? She brought him a large vodka, and he smiled, 'That's better.' Watching her walk back to the house, he said, 'She is a beauty.' I tapped his knee, 'Never mind the scenery, what have you got for me.' He sent the vodka over his throat in one move, then pulled out a paper bag.

He took out a dozen pictures, one showed John standing outside a gay club, speaking to a couple of guys, and another photo showed him with his arm around a young guy.

'Sorry mate, but your friend is gay.' I gave him a hundred dollars, he put the photos on the table and left.

Alice sat down, everything all right?

I showed her the photos, and she laughed saying, 'Who is going to tell Monica?' I paused and said, 'Nobody, he is holding a half-million dollars of my money, let's not upset the setup, if the guy is gay, I think Monica will figure it out soon enough, and I think Monica will speak to me if she has any doubts, so let's not say anything just yet.'

We all went to John's car dealership on Saturday, Monica had made up one of her girls to the salon manager. She now had seven girls working at the salon and could take things a little easier.

We sat in a big office with a huge desk and were surrounded by pictures of Maserati, Bentleys and Aston Martins. John brought in a tray of coffee and sandwiches, he sounded happy and said, 'When we finish our coffee, I will show you around the cars.

The garage and forecourt were filled with new and late model cars, Cadillacs, Lincolns and some American muscle cars. It all looked very impressive. I reckoned a Million dollars of metal. John showed us around the shiny expensive cars, and said, 'That Cadillac that you have at the house, I will give you a good deal on a new one.

I smiled, putting my hand on a new car I said,

'You could not buy that car for a million bucks.'

The girls went off chatting to the young sales guys, John said,

'If our business deal with the money works out, I am going to open another garage, would you be interested in investing?

I looked around the modern showroom at the high-end cars.

'Well, let's see how things work out first, but yes, I would be interested.' When the girls came back into the showroom, John put his arm around Monica and kissed her. Alice giggled and winked at me. I shook my head and put a finger to my lips.

Back at the house, Pedro, the Mexican gardener was working in the flower beds, Alice shouted,

'Do you want me to help you, Pedro,' He shook his head,

'No, no, maybe later, later!

Andy rang me from Los Angeles, he told me that he had to pay out a few bribes to cops and that his legal office was getting so much work that he hired a newly qualified lawyer to help out with the legal side of things so that he could work with Albie on the hash business, which was booming. He said, I am also getting married, so you will have an invitation It'll be an excuse for you to visit Los Angeles.

Pedro, the Mexican hash supplier rang me, to say that he was coming up to Miami to discuss the price of hash. He had said this before but never turned up.

I had read about the drug wars in Mexico but had assumed it was all about the cocaine trade, as the profit on cocaine was ten times more than the profit on hash, plus the Mexican cops didn't have the manpower or the inclination to chase the hash trade.

While the American government was paying the Mexican cops to chase the cocaine gangs, the cocaine gangs were paying the cops to leave them alone, so the Americans had permission to send down special forces to bring down the big gangs.

Pedro had told me that as long as he only dealt in the hash, the cops, for a small bribe, left him alone to trade, but that the raw materials to make hash had gone up in price, so he had to pass it along. Was that true? Or was he just trying to hustle for more money, trouble was, he had never let me down with the quality of the hash, and the deliveries were always on time. I had heard of horror stories, where you would send the cash and never hear from them again, or the hash was mixed with camel shit, and then you would lose your reputation and customers.

I always said to my contacts, never overcharge or mess with the hash, or you will be gone. I had a good setup with Andy and Albie, they did all the organizing in Los Angeles, and I made sure that they got the hash, and got a good percentage of the profits. I could have made more money, but as long as I got my cut every month, why be greedy I had millions anyway, and a great life in the sunshine.

We often dined out with Monica and John, he would ask,

'What do you do for a living? I would make up different things like my great aunt had left me millions or that I was a banker and made it big on the shares, he didn't believe the tales, so he would ask Monica, and she told him that Moe, my business partner had been murdered and had left his estate and money to me. He settled for that version.

He said that he saw a garage for sale that would be perfect to expand the car business, it was a few miles down the coast highway.

'Yes, I nodded, let's have a look tomorrow.' The next morning, Alice, Monica John and I all got into a huge classic open-top Lincoln convertible and drove down the beautiful coastal highway.

We pulled up at a huge empty car showroom, just off the highway. The building had a long frontage.

A tall pale-faced guy was waiting for us, it was ninety degrees in the shade, but the tall guy was wearing a coat and hat. He led us into the showroom, then the offices and the mechanic's bay. Everything seemed in order. The thin guy told us that his partner had been caught bringing cocaine into Miami from Mexico, he got ten years in jail, and that his partner was the money man, who had left a trail of debts with the garage. So, he had to sell before the bank foreclosed, then he would get zilch. We agreed on a price subject to a few inquiries, we shook hands with the guy and left.

We pulled into a restaurant off the highway and overlooking the beach. We all sat outside with a drink. John was excited,

'What do you think?' 'I tried not to look too satisfied,

'Yes, it looks good, but let me have a few guys that I know look into the garage—and the guy.

As John went to the bar for more drinks, the girls came over, Monica was grinning when she held up her right hand, she had a diamond ring on her third finger, both girls were grinning, Alice started singing in her terrible voice,

'We're going to the chaaapel, and we're going to get maaarried.' John came back carrying the drinks, Alice laughed,

'A nice ring. I'll need to buy another dress,—and a hat.'

John kissed Monica and looked around at everyone,

'This is the girl for me.' Monica looked at me, pressed her finger to her lips and fluttered her eyelashes.

On the phone the next morning, I spoke with the lawyer about the garage and the tall thin guy, he said it would take a few days to check him out. The surveyor said he would do a check if he could get the keys. And my cop friend would look if the guy had form.

CHAPTER 13

Alice and I were having breakfast on the patio when the front door buzzer went, Alice went to the door and came back with Pedro my hash supplier. I hugged him and said, 'Want some coffee buddy? he sat at the table and told me a long story about the local Mexican cops shaking all the hash dealers down because the cocaine dealers were suffering from the American special forces closing down their jungle laboratories, and we're not liaising with the Mexican cops anymore, then the cops could not warn the dealers when the next raid was going to happen.

So, the cocaine dealers had stopped the bribes, and the cops had turned to the hash dealers to make up their losses, hence the price of hash had to go up to pay the bribes.

Pedro reckoned that a ten per cent rise would cover the cost of the bribes. Pedro smiled as he lifted his cup,

'That's how business is done in Mexico, everyone has their finger in the pie.' I agreed on the extra ten per cent. I would have to tell Andy and Albie in Los Angeles. That the price has gone up. I knew that all the other hash dealers would be in the same boat, so I wouldn't lose any customers.

Pedro stayed a couple of days, we took him to a plush restaurant and a club that we sometimes went to, he loved all the attention. One evening Alice and I went to see Monica, she had moved into John's huge ranch-style bungalow, with security gates that didn't work When we arrived at the bungalow we had to ring to tell him we were waiting outside. John came out in the rain and had to pull the gates open, Then cursed.

Monica was cooking a meal and talking to Alice in the kitchen.

John was showing me some paperwork, showing that he had bought and paid for several cars. He said, 'Most of these cars are already sold before they even get here. Then asked, Any news on the coast garage?' I shook my head;

'We will have some news by the weekend.'

On the drive back Alice said,

'Are you sure this guy is gay? Monica told me that he is a tiger in bed and not a pussy cat. We both laughed,

At the house, Pedro had left and there was a note on the table, it said thanks for showing him a nice time, and why don't we come down to his house in Mexico. Alice made coffee and brought it to the patio, then we got into the pool. It was lovely and cool, making the problems melt away.

In the morning Alice came back into the bedroom and said,

'You had better come downstairs. We have a guest.' We both went to the kitchen, there was a girl with long blond hair making toast. wearing a men's shirt I stood behind Alice as she asked,

'Who the hell are you? The blond smiled,

'I am with Pedro,' Alice shook her head,

'Pedro has gone.' The girl stopped smiling and shook her head,

'Then who is going to pay my fee, I don't give my services for free.' I burst out laughing,

'I'll have to take it out of Pedro's next payment.'

The blond girl joined us for breakfast on the patio and we got talking. She told us that she had a husband in a wheelchair and two young kids to feed. She said that Pedro had promised her five hundred dollars to come back to the house and "entertain" him.

I gave her five hundred dollars, then put her in a taxi. Alice showed me the girl's card with the number that she had left on the patio table. It said, "Need a girlfriend for an hour? Ring......!"

The surveyor rang and told me that apart from some minor repairs the building was sound. Then the lawyer rang me the same day, he said that there was a fifteen thousand loan against the building from a bank and that the sale couldn't happen until the loan was repaid. I spoke with John and the skinny guy and arranged a meeting with the bank. At the bank, the loan was bought for fifteen thousand dollars, and then we all went to the lawyer's office to agree on a sale document for the garage. We agreed on three hundred thousand dollars. Then went to John's car showroom to celebrate. Over drinks, John huddled with Monica talking about colour schemes.

Another one million was put into the new garage for cars from Mexico to fill the showroom and outside areas, the offices were refurbished. In the first month of trading, we cleared over one million dollars in sales. One of the sales team from the old garage was put in to train the new sales team of three guys. We put in a top-of-the-range coffee machine with a table and chairs for the customers. John asked Alice to work at the new garage as a hostess, showing the potential customers around and introducing them to the sales guys, she loved the attention and was there every weekend,

I would drive her to the garage and stay for a coffee and a chat with John. Alice was speaking with customers and flirting with the sales guys.

The two garages needed over a million dollars a month to buy the cars from Mexico to stock the two garages, and I was getting almost one and a half million in return, everybody was making money. Monica was hiring another two hairdressers for the salon and asked me to come with her to look at another salon by the beach.

John gave Monica and Alice cars to use from the garage showroom, Monica chose a small family hatchback and Alice picked out a red two-door Maserati soft-top sports model.

One warm evening, Alice and I took a drive in her Maserati along the coast. She loved to drive that car with the top down and her hair blowing in the wind, and I liked to see her smile with those perfect white teeth. We drove past the new garage when I saw a couple of guys doing something with one of the cars that was still on the back of the car transporter. I asked Alice to turn around and go back to the garage. We pulled up at the garage forecourt, the light was fading but I saw that they had taken a wheel off one of the cars. I got out and walked over to the guys, 'What are you doing guys?'

A tall thin guy with a bandana and an earring said,

'Get lost man.' Looking over his shoulder I saw that the other guy was taking little parcels out of the tyre—Drugs. They had been taking drugs over the border from Mexico hidden in the car tyres. I wondered if John was involved. The thin guy then punched me; I fell to the ground dazed.

Alice was helping me to stand up. She told me that they had collected the parcels and drove off. Back at the house I rang John and told him all about the drama at the garage, he swore that it had nothing to do with him, I didn't know if I believed him.

We agreed to meet at the Garage in the morning. I rang Monica at the salon and asked her if John had any visitors the day before, she said that she was at the salon, but that he had people coming and going all the time.

Alice drove me to the garage on the coast highway, the car transporter was still there, and the mechanics were unloading the cars, John came out of the garage with his manager, who said,

'We have a night watchman. I asked,

'Where was he when this was happening.' John waved a hand,

'He probably has taken a bribe, I'll fire him.'

The manager nodded and told us the same thing happened last delivery, when we opened the garage up in the morning, one of the cars that were sitting on the car transporter had a wheel off, we just thought that someone was stealing a wheel, when we spoke to the night watchman, he said he felt ill and went home early. John said,

'It all adds up, the night watchman is in with the drug smugglers.' Alice nodded,

'If the customs guys at the border find drugs in the cars, you know whom they are going to suspect!' we all agreed.

The address of the night watchman was a mobile home.

He was sitting outside on a plastic chair when I drove up.

'Want a beer man?' I put my thumb up, he shouted at someone on the mobile, and a grey-haired woman came out followed by three cats and gave me a cold beer, we clinked bottles and took a swig,

he said, 'How can I help you, young man? I took another swig,

'You can start by telling me who is paying you to disappear when the car transporters arrive.' He went quiet, shuffled his boots in the dust, took a swig of beer and said,

'It was just a coincidence.' Then took another drink. I gave him a moment to think, then said,

'You can tell me or speak to the cops, what's it to be?' The grey-haired woman standing in the doorway said,

'Tell him, we don't want the cops coming here with your record.' The guy growled; 'They gave me fifty bucks to get lost when the car transporters arrived from Mexico.' I handed him my empty bottle.

'Who are they, and where can I find them?' The old woman went into the Mobile followed by the cats, and came out and handed the old man a notebook and a pen.

I parked outside the house, walked through the door and into the kitchen, two Mexicans were sitting smoking hash, and playing Loteria, a card game. One guy dropped his cards and pulled a knife from his pocket, it was the same guy that I had seen taking drug parcels from the wheel at the garage, the same guy with the bandana and earrings when Alice had driven me there. He said something to his friend in Spanish, who got up from the table and walked up to me, then started patting me down.

I punched him on the side of the head, and he collapsed onto the floor. The guy with the knife ran towards me, I dodged to the side of the table picked up a chair and hit his arm, he let go of the knife, then as he bent down to pick it up, I hit him again with the chair, knocking him out cold.

Tying them both to chairs and splashing water on their faces they came around. I put the knife against his throat, I said,

'I have to kill the one who is slow to tell me the whole story,' they both started talking at once. Their Mexican supplier would tell them when the cars were due to arrive, and the model of the car with the drugs on board.

I had killed enough guys, so I told them to tell their supplier to get another place to deliver the drugs, tell them we are watching the car transporters as they arrive, and that we will keep the drugs, they nodded their heads. I put the knife on the table and walked out.

John nodded when I told him what had happened. That weekend the garage was mobbed with people. It had a carnival atmosphere. Not sure if it was the cars, the free coffee or the beautiful Alice that they came for. The money was still coming in from the hash in Los Angeles, and the investments with the old guy and his sons, and now the garage business.

Monica's Wedding was a lavish affair on the beach, John introduced Alice and me to his only brother. The guy was as gay as you can be, with eyeliner, peroxide blond hair and waving a pink hanky about. He spoke and acted like a raving poof. Alice danced with him and was laughing her head off. She said later,

'That explains the photos of John at the gay club, he had gone there to see his brother!'

We drank champagne and listened to the speeches, howled at the jokes, and danced till the band took a break, and then Monica waved goodbye, and they were off to Hawaii for a week. Alice said that John had asked her to be at the garage every day to keep an eye on things, till he got back.

We took a taxi back to the house, stripped off and got into the pool to cool down. Alice was drunk as she hugged me and said,

'When I got into the pool, I wanted a pee, she smiled, I don't need one now,' she laughed. In the dark I didn't notice the guy standing at the edge of the pool, pointing a gun, till he laughed too, Alice screamed and moved behind me.

'What do you want,' I shouted, he grinned,

'Just here to give you a warning. Don't interfere with the drugs on the car transporters.' I pointed to my ears and shouted,

'I can't hear you, I'll get out of the pool and put my hearing aid in,' Alice said, 'Yes, he can't hear a thing.' We both got out of the pool, Alice and I were both starkers. I went over to the patio table, turned my back on the guy and fiddled with an imaginary hearing aid. He stood next to me as she walked past, he was getting an eyeful of Alice as I grabbed the gun and punched him hard, he fell on his knees dazed, I punched him again and he dropped to the patio floor. Alice said, 'What did you hit him again for? I smiled,

'For staring at my naked girlfriend.' She laughed, and said,

'Are you jealous?'

We tied him to a chair and got dressed, Alice made coffee and sat with me at the table when the guy came around, I put the gun on the table and Alice untied him and gave him a cup of coffee, he looked at me and spat out,

'I'll have you and your bitch, fed to the pigs, don't mess with me.'

In his jacket pocket was a local phone number, I asked,

'Who is this? He growled,

'Why don't you ring and find out?' I untied him and sat down, here is your gun, now get out of my house.

He slowly picked his gun up and stepped back from the table, smiling, he said, 'You're a bigger fool than I could have imagined, stand up sucker,' he fired his gun, and there were two clicks, he stared at the gun, I pulled my gun from under the table, opened my hand and threw five bullets on the table,

'I think these are yours?' He swore and threw his gun at me, I dodged the gun and shot him. Alice screamed and turned her head away; I stepped over and shot him again.

I dragged his body to the garage, then mopped the blood from the patio tiles. In the morning, I told Alice to say nothing that had happened the night before, then kissed a nervous Alice goodbye as she drove off to the garage.

Putting the body into the boot of the Cadillac I drove along the coast freeway. Pulled up at a remote spot near the cliffs, took the body out of the boot threw it over the cliff, and watched as it disappeared into the sea. Watching the body sink, I didn't feel any guilt or remorse, he was going to shoot me and he would have to get rid of Alice,

who would tell the cops if he had let her live?

The phone number in the guy's jacket was local. I rang my cop friend, and gave him the number, he said to give him ten minutes. My phone rang, and I had an address.

I parked on the driveway of a big suburban mansion, and a big fat, bald guy was standing outside smoking and watching the gardener prune some trees, I would recognize that face anywhere.

'Hi, Charlie.' He waved, and took me into the kitchen while he made coffee,

'What do you want?' I smiled,

'I was just passing, and I thought I would pop in and say hi.'

We sat at the kitchen table, Charlie smiled,

'What are you here for?

'Charlie, why did you send a gunman to my house to give me the warning to lay off the drug guys?' Charlie slowly stirred his coffee, then smiling said,

'That was a little side-line of mine, and you messed it up. Where is the guy that I sent to your house?' I finished my coffee and stood;

'He is with the fishes. Charlie, don't mess with my business and I won't mess with your business, understood? He nodded his head.

Monica and John were back from Hawaii, looking fit and tanned, Monica hugged me and said,

'I am so glad to be back, I missed you and Alice.' The girls sat by the coffee bar and were deep in conversation with the occasional burst of laughter. John led me into one of the small sales offices and we sat down and I told him about the visit with Charlie.

'I don't think we will be hassled by the drug guys anymore.

I told him about the visit by the gunman to my house, but I didn't tell him that he was now swimming with the fish.

Alice was sworn to be secretive about the whole visit.

The old guy with his two sons asked me to meet at the hotel to discuss an investment idea. At the hotel, we shook hands all around. The old man pushed a case across the table, and said,

'Here is your share from your last investment.'

The case was full of cash.

We were joined by a shady-looking older guy, dressed like a Mafia gangster, in a black suit, shirt and tie. With black and white shoes, and wearing dark shades, when he smiled, he showed a mouthful of gold teeth, was he an extra from a gangster movie?

One of the sons said,

'This is Don Marchetti, the owner of a string of pasta restaurants, he is looking for a Four-million-dollar loan to expand his chain. Don Marchetti smiled, showing a mouthful of gold teeth,

'Grazie, Grazie.'

'What's the return?' I asked, 'And more importantly, what kind of guarantees can you give me.' Don Marchetti stood up,

'You insult me, my word is your guarantee.' Then sat down.

I looked at him, and said,

'You came to me for the loan, I need some guarantees before I part with Four million dollars.'

He wrote out a list of addresses across the Florida state, then threw the sheet across the table.

'Here, he spat out, check out my businesses.' The old guy hadn't said a word, Don Marchetti stood up shook hands, and said,

'I am a busy guy. I've got to go. Then turned to me and said, 'I'll want your decision by the end of the week.'

After the door was closed, the old guy said,

'He is not one of our regular clients, it is the people behind him that pulls the strings, but it's up to you if you want to do a deal with Mr. Marchetti.' I picked up my case with the cash and left.

Alice got all dressed up, and we drove to one of the pasta restaurants on the list that Don Marchetti had given me. The place was full, we were sat at a table, and a young Italian waiter came over, then after glancing down the front of Alice's dress, he asked what we would like to eat. We ordered a chicken and spaghetti dish with a bottle of chianti, he poured some of the wine into Alice's glass first, and she gave him her best smile. I tapped him on the arm and said,

'When you are finished, do you think I can have some wine?'

Alice giggled, and the waiter looked flushed,

'Sorry sir.' As he poured out my wine, I whispered to him,

'Don't waste your time, you couldn't afford her.'

After we finished the meal, I went to the toilet. A cook was leaning against the wall having a smoke, I said,

'Nice place you have here,' he blew smoke and smiled,

'Not for long, the place is in deep trouble, it owes money to the suppliers, and I haven't been paid this month.' As I paid the bill, Alice grinned and said, 'Give our waiter a good tip, I pulled a face,

'Alice, behave yourself.'

I rang my private eye and asked him to sniff around a few of the Restaurants on the list, let me know what you can find out before the end of the week.

I sat at the table with the old guy and his sons, chatting, when Don Marchetti walked in and sat, we shook hands. Then he asked,

'When do I get the money?' I stared for a moment then said,

'OK, but something isn't Kosher. The food was good, and the service was fast, but I heard a rumour that some of the waiters had not been paid that month and a few suppliers had stopped deliveries because the bills were late. Also, you have put some of the restaurants up for sale. 'Don Marchetti jumped up, and shook his fist, 'What lying son of a bitch who told you that, I'll kill him with my bare hands.' Suddenly he pulled a gun from his belt.

The old man put his hands up and his two sons dived under the table. I put my hands up and said, 'Shooting me won't get you that loan, but it will get you twenty years to life in the penitentiary.'

Don Marchetti slumped into the chair and put his gun on the table. One of the old man's sons grabbed the gun off the table. Then the old man put his arm around Don Marchetti.

The Don said that he had been paying protection money

for the last ten years and it had ruined the business. He told me that he paid two thousand dollars in protection money every Friday at his restaurant on the coast highway. 'I said,

'If I can get the protection guys off your back, would the restaurants survive? He nodded, I shook his hand and said, 'I'll be in touch.'

Sitting in the restaurant, the one off the coast highway, the place was half empty when two guys walked in and sat at a table, after a few minutes Don Marchetti came from the kitchen dressed in chefs' whites, handed a small bag to one of the guys and without a word having been said, walked back into the kitchen.

The black Cadillac pulled out of the car park, with me a little way behind, twenty minutes later it stopped at an apartment block, the two guys got into a lift, and I rushed right behind them into the lift before the doors closed. We all stood in silence as the lift went up the floors.

There was a strong smell of cologne. When the lift stopped and the guys got out, I followed, they knocked three times on a door, I walked past, and at the end of the lobby, I made a mental note of the floor and the door number. I sat in the reception area with a newspaper watching people come and go, and then the two guys and another tall, well-dressed guy came out of the lift and walked to the Cadillac.

I rang my cop friend with the registration of the Cadillac and got the name and address of the owner. The house was by the ocean, a million-dollar house surrounded by other million-dollar houses, in a very exclusive area.

The gates were open, and some kind of party was going on.

I joined the crowd, grabbing a glass of champagne from a passing waiter's tray.

'It's his wife's birthday, a purple-haired drunk woman told me,

Through her laughter, she said, 'She is forty,—again!—her daughter is thirty-two.'

she held my arm as tears ran down her ruddy cheeks.

Looking around the crowd, I saw one of the guys that were in the lift speaking to an old grey-haired guy, with a long red scar on his cheek. I hid behind a couple so I would not be recognized. I asked a waiter who Scarface was, and he seemed surprised,

'Why it's Mr Cappello, are you not one of his employees?'

One of the people that owed me a favour was an ex-safecracker. Arranging to meet him, I knew he had just been released from jail, and was probably broke. I was sitting at the bar, when he tapped me on the shoulder, and then hugged me, like a long-lost friend. I got the drinks and we sat in one of the alcoves. He stared at the glass before picking it up and saying, 'First drink in four years,' then sent the drink over his throat.' Wiping his mouth with the back of his hand he said, 'What can I do for you, my friend?

Over drinks I told him that I needed a stick of TNT with a fuse, he said, 'You have been watching too many gangster movies

It's all technology now, I can get you the latest in bang bangs. What's it for?' I smiled,

'To scare the crows off my land, he put his head to one side,

'I don't want to know, I was asking because there are different strengths, I nodded,

'Let's say, to blow a car over a wall.'

We met at the weekend in the same bar, sitting in an alcove, he opened a bag and put a small box and a TV remote onto the table. He showed me how to flick a switch on the box, then which button to press on the remote, then said smiling,

'Are we even now?' I gave him two hundred bucks and left.

On Friday I sat at the same table in the Pasta restaurant, I had spoken to Don Marchetti and put some cut-up newspaper in a box with the explosive that I had super glued shut. The same two guys came in and sat at the same table, Don Marchetti came from the kitchen and handed them the box, wrapped in a paper bag, then walked back into the kitchen. No words were spoken.

The Cadillac drove through the gates and up the driveway to the house, there was still enough daylight to see into the lounge, sitting outside the iron gates with my binoculars.

Sitting at a table was Scarface, he took the box from the two guys and then struggled to get it open. One of the guys produced a knife and handed the knife to Scarface.

I pulled off the newspaper covering the remote and pressed the button.

The blast blew the lounge window into the garden, the curtains were on fire and there was smoke billowing through what was the front window. I turned the key and drove off, past a few people looking through the iron gates at the carnage.

Alice drove me to the pasta restaurant, Don Marchetti came through from the kitchen, I introduced him to Alice, then told him, I had spoken to the boss of the protection guys, I said, 'That the meeting went with a bang,' And I convinced them not to bother you again, I then handed him a bag with five thousand dollars,

'This will help to pay your waiters and the suppliers.'

Don Marchetti took my hand and kissed it.

'I will pay you back and more, there were tears in his eyes, I patted his shoulder and said, 'No need my friend, but I might ask you for a favour in the future.' He squeezed my hand,

'Anything, anytime,' We sat at the table and ordered pasta and wine, Don Marchetti served us himself, fussing around Alice and me, going from the kitchen to our table with the food.

I went to the desk to pay the bill, but Don Marchetti rushed over and tore the bill up,

'You will always be my guests to dine here, and never be asked to pay.' We waved goodbye and drove off.

I drove over to Scarface's house, the builders were putting the finishing touches to the damage, I knocked on the door, and an old woman dressed all in black wearing a diamond neckless said,

'Yes, how can I help,' I told her I was a friend of Mr Cappello,

'I am sorry for your loss,' She opened the door wider,

'Come in.' In the huge musty lounge, she motioned me to join her sitting on a huge settee she said, 'Would you like a drink, I nodded, I would love a whisky. Mrs Cappello shouted,

'Greta come now.' A thin young girl with a sad face walked into the room, Mrs Cappello said, 'A large whisky with ice, and I'll have my usual.' Greta returned with a tray, on it was a large whisky with ice

a bottle of gin and a glass. Mrs Cappello waved Greta away saying,

'Silly girl she forgot the tonic, O well, never mind. She poured herself a large gin. Taking a long sip and burping, she said,

'My husband left me a wealthy woman, and although we had our problems, I think he loved me,' the door opened and in walked a well-dressed, young woman. She nodded, then said,

'Mother, is there anything that you would like me to bring back from town? Mrs Cappello introduced the woman as her daughter.

'Will you stay for dinner, young man,' I nodded a yes, and said,

'I would like that.' As we sat drinking, she talked about the early days, when Mr. Cappello would disappear for two or three days and return with a bag of money.

She shook her head;

'I still don't know what he did for a living.' In the middle of talking, she leaned back into the couch, fell asleep, and began to snore loudly. I waited until I was sure she was asleep.

Then went upstairs and found the office,

going through the filing cabinets were files with names, one of the files had the name, Don Marchetti. The file had the names and addresses of his restaurants and the name of one of his employees.

The other files had the names and addresses of shops, businesses and an ice cream vendor. These were all places that he was getting protection money from. I stuck everything into a bag and went downstairs. Mrs Cappello had slipped halfway off the settee and was still holding her glass. With the gin spilt over her dress.

Greta came into the room and announced that the soup had been served. Sitting at the huge dining table, Greta stood behind me as I slurped my soup, she took my bowl away, and came back with a prawn salad and a glass of white wine. I said, 'Sit down and join me, Greta.'

She glanced through to the lounge and whispered,

'Madam does not let me sit at the table. I have my meals at the kitchen table.' I said, 'Look Greta, Madam is out cold for the duration, sit down and join me. Greta crept to the open door looked in the lounge, then came back and sat down next to me.

She told me that Scarface was a monster who would get drunk and smash things, everybody had to get out of his way till he passed out, and when he got blown up nobody shed a tear.

Greta's face broke into a smile when she told me that the police said he had so many enemies that they didn't know where to start looking. I finished the meal.

'Greta, tell Mrs Cappello how much I enjoyed the food and her hospitality, but I had to attend to my business.'

At the house, I went through the list of names and picked one out. Got into my car and drove to one of the addresses. It was an office, at the reception desk, the girl put me through to the name on the list. I sat down in the plush office, the guy behind the desk lit up a cigar,

'What do you want to talk about?'

Leaning forward, I waved the smoke away and said,

'How about protection money?' The guy put his cigar down leaned, into the leather chair and muttered,

'Go on, I am listening!' I said, 'What if I can get the protection guys out of your life?' He laughed and picked up his cigar paused and said, 'Let's say you can stop them threatening me, How much?' I smiled, 'I don't want your money, but I might want a favour in the future,' I passed him a file with a photograph of him with a girl naked. He looked at the picture for a full minute, then said,

'Are there any copies?' Shaking my head,

'No that's it, so I am saving your marriage and five thousand dollars a month, he looked at me for a moment,

'What's the catch?'

'No catch, but you owe me a favour, I might call for it in the future,' I stood up and left him staring at the photo.

The next one on the list was an ice cream vendor, the van was in a park playing musical chimes. He was a large overweight guy with a bald head and glasses. I handed him the file with his name on it, he said, 'What's this?' then looked inside and started to weep,

'What do you want, I can't afford any more.'

I scratched my head. 'I'll settle for a double cone with a chocolate fudge topping.'

Number three was a cop. I drove up his driveway. He was in the front garden talking with a woman and watering the lawn. Stepping out of the car, and walking towards the pair, I said, 'Can we talk in private? The guy glanced at the woman,'

'You can say whatever you want, I have no secrets from my wife.' He smiled at her and she took his arm. I asked,

'Do you know a Don Cappello?' Turning off the hose he said, 'Darling, make a coffee for the man.' He walked closer to me.

'If this is a shakedown, I would rather go to jail than pay anymore.' I handed him the file, and he went silent and said,

'How much?'

'Nothing, the coffee is enough.' the woman came out of the house with two coffees. She had a worried look and asked,

'Everything all right darling?'

he nodded, and we drank our coffee in silence, I handed the cup to his wife,

'Thanks, but I must get going,' looking at the cop, I said,

'You owe me a favour, right? He nodded. His wife said,

'What is this all about, honey? They were still talking as I left.

CHAPTER 14

I felt as if I had earned my way to get through the gates of heaven.

Sitting on the patio in my shorts and Hawaiian shirt, with a glass of black label Johnnie Walker whisky and ice, watching my lovely Alice, swimming in the pool naked. What could go wrong?

I took Alice with me to the wedding of Andy and his girlfriend, Sally, in Los Angeles. Albie and his not-so-skinny wife were there, he told me how the hash business was growing every month, and how Andy was organizing everything, so, apart from some bribes that had to be paid out to the cops, the business was running like clockwork. Andy spoke with me, saying,

'Your girlfriend is a beauty.' He said that Albie and his family went on their first-ever vacation to Florida, he told me they had never seen the ocean. His son had said to him, that when they saw the tide starting to go out, he thought it would keep going back and disappear. We both laughed.

Albie drove Alice and me to the Airport and said their goodbyes, he thanked me for his new life, and said, 'Do you still remember when we first met, and you gave me my, then skinny wife some cash to buy coffee and paid the mortgage arrears?' He shook my hand, then went back to his car with a wave. The flight was delayed for a couple of hours, so we sat at the bar drinking, Alice with her champagne and me with the black label Johnnie Walker and ice. Heaven!

Back in the sunshine of Miami, I rang Don Marchetti and told him the name of one of his employees who was giving information about his business to the protection gang. Don Marchetti was furious. He shouted, 'I treated that son of a bitch like my own son, and he betrays me, his father was my cousin, and he will disgrace his family for this betrayal.' I had decided to settle in Miami, now I needed a wife and Alice fitted the bill, smart, beautiful, and a perfect hostess.

I met with Monica in a restaurant, and as we sat having a meal, I told Monica that I was going to propose to Alice. Monica dropped her fork and let out a little scream.

'George, Alice has been in love with you for ages,'

'Let me ring and give her the news, Monica was excited, I put up my hand,

'No Monica, we will all go to a restaurant tonight and I will propose, but for now, let's go and find a nice diamond ring.' Monica leapt up from the table,

'Come on let's go.' We shopped at the most expensive diamond centre store in Miami. We sat on a large plush sofa, assistants brought champagne, and two guys in sharp suits showed us trays of diamond rings, Monica picked one, put it on her finger, and then went and stood by a mirror with the guys at her side, I was left on the sofa. Monica sat back on the sofa; and said,

'This is the one,' the guys fussed over her, one guy said,

'Your fiancé has great taste. Monica giggled;

'I am not the fiancé.' I took a deep breath,

'OK, how much for the ring.' Monica muttered,

'I think you had better sit down first.' One of the guys looked at the tag on the ring,

'It's only two hundred and fifty thousand dollars. I stared.

'Jesus, I thought you said two hundred and fifty thousand.' I took a deep breath, then pulled out my mobile phone and transferred the money, put the ring in my pocket and stepped outside for fresh air. Monica was still buzzing,

'Where shall we meet?'

Back at the house, Alice was in the pool. I sat at the patio table with a drink. When she came out and wrapped a beach towel around her I told her we were meeting Monica and John for a meal,

she sat drying her hair and nodded.

I would love to go out for a meal with those guys. We met at the pasta restaurant, Monica and John were grinning. Alice whispered, 'What are you two so happy about? Monica, are you pregnant?'

They both shook their heads at the same time and carried on smiling.

Alice stood up to visit the toilet. Monica jumped up but was pulled back into her chair by John,

'You will tell her. You are so excited.' Alice came back and we finished our meal. I ordered a bottle of champagne.

We all lifted our glasses, Alice looked a little puzzled and said,

'What are we celebrating? I put my glass on the table, got down on one knee, and pulled the diamond ring from my pocket.

'Will you marry me, Alice? She dropped her glass, put her hands to her cheeks and started to cry. Monica was crying and hugging Alice. The people sitting in the restaurant began to clap and cheer. 'Well Alice? Monica shouted, 'Yes George yes, she will marry you.'

We all went back to the house. John and I sat at the patio table with drinks and talking about the garage business, the girls were in the pool chattering nonstop. Alice kept looking at the ring and hugging Monica.

Alice and Monica were going to make all the arrangements for the wedding.

John and I had to go down to Mexico to sort out a problem with the car deliveries. We landed at Guadalajara, a car was at the Airport to pick us up and take us to a hotel. After twenty minutes of driving, John asked the driver, how far is it to this hotel, the driver said nothing, and ten minutes later we drove into a large farmyard. Three masked men with guns came to the car and said, 'Get out hombres.' They took us into a barn and tied us to chairs, and then a short fat guy with a beard and a baseball cap came into the barn.

'Hello, hombres, welcome to Mexico.'

the guys in the masks laughed. The fat guy lit a cigarette, and said,

'Gentlemen. If you want to see Miami, and your lovely wives again, you will present me with half a million dollars, we know you can afford to lose that amount, your company spends a million a month buying cars. Or else, we will cut you up into small pieces and send you back to Miami. It will be half a million bucks or say goodbye to your very profitable life, what's your choice gents?' The fat guy and the gunmen left the barn and closed the door. What went wrong?

John shook his head, and said, 'Our contact at the car delivery company had double-crossed us or been scared off.' After fifteen minutes the door opened again, and the fat guy came in with two masked men and a tray of coffee. We were untied but told to stay in the chairs.

'Times up, what's it going to be.' I took a sip of coffee,

'OK, you can have the money, but how do I know that you will let us go, the fat man smiled,

'Why should we kill you if we have the money, that will tarnish my reputation,' He raised his voice.

'One of you will go back to Miami for the cash, if he is not back here in one week with the money, we will send the other one back in small parcels.' I was chosen to go back to Miami, I said goodbye to John, then the masked guys put me into the car, and we drove out of the farmyard. It was too late for a flight to Miami, so I booked into a hotel near the Airport, and then took a taxi to police headquarters, at the desk I asked to speak to someone in charge. While I was waiting for the cop to come back with someone. I looked through the office window, there at a desk, speaking to another cop was the short fat guy with the beard, sitting at a desk with the words inspector on a sign at the front of his desk.

A taxi was waiting outside the police headquarters. At the hotel, I spoke to two shady-looking characters. We all got into a car and drove to another hotel. In the lift, one of the guys said,

'Have you got money to pay my friend?' In the room were four guys and a woman drinking and playing cards. We shook hands with guys at the table, then a small thin guy took me into another room, smiling through missing teeth he said, 'Show me the money,' I nodded, 'You show me the goods.' He opened a drawer next to the bed and took out a forty-five revolver. I checked it for bullets, then handed him two hundred dollars.

I described the journey to the farmyard, and the woman at the table nodded, 'It is the old farm that once belonged to my cousin.' She offered to show me the way for one hundred dollars.

I climbed into her car and set off. It was pitch black when she stopped the car a hundred yards from the farm. The farm was in darkness as we both crept up to the gates. She wanted to come with me, she said that she knew the farm inside out as she played there as a kid.

We walked in the darkness to a small door in the fence. Once inside the yard, I recognized the outline of the barn. I crept up to a window and looked inside. John was playing cards with one guy; another guy was sleeping on a straw bed with his rifle at the bottom of the bed. The guy playing cards with John had a gun on the table next to him.

The woman whispered that there was a door at the back of the barn. In the darkness, we slowly walked round to the back of the barn, the door creaked when I opened it. The guy playing cards with John turned around and said something in Spanish, then carried on playing cards. Creeping to the table I put my gun to the guy's head. he froze. John grabbed his gun from the table. then stood and took the rifle from the sleeping beauty. After tying them to the chairs, we made our way in the darkness back to the woman's car. I gave her another hundred dollars to take us to the Airport.

We spent the rest of the night in the hotel bar. In the morning I rang the American consulate and told a guy there what had happened, he said to wait at the bar and he would send some of his staff to record the story that I had just told him.

The staff arrived with a high-ranking Mexican police chief who listened to my story. He nodded; 'I believe you but without proof, there is nothing that I can do.' John spoke to his contact in the car business, they knew nothing about a meeting, they told him that someone with access to their office had sent the message to come to Mexico.

The flight back to Miami was a discussion on security and a promise never to go back to that country again, ever. The girls picked us up from the Airport.

We drove to John's Bungalow, where his Mexican cook served up chicken and beans, Mexican style, washed down with beer.

The girls were excited to tell us what they had planned for the wedding on the beach.

Andy rang to say that there had been a police raid on the warehouse and that the entire stock had been taken, I said, 'What about the cops we had bribed to give us warning of potential raids?' Andy went on, the police had set up a special squad to raid drug houses, and a new chief of police had been appointed to rid the city of drug barons, they didn't share the knowledge with the other departments, so now we could not be warned of a coming raid. We spoke about finding a cop who was on the special squad and finding out who we could bribe. We discussed making good on the loss, I rang Pedro in Mexico and arranged a shipment to Los Angeles to make up the loss.

John and I discussed the possibility of opening another Garage, but he was nervous about that idea, saying that if we relied on our whole operation by getting the cars from Mexico, what would we do if the Mexican operation fell through? He said, 'You know the level of corruption and bribery to get anything done, we don't want to count on everything going smoothly forever, we need another source to supply us with cheap cars.'

Monica and I drove up to a beauty shop in the hills in the suburbs of Miami, the shop was surrounded by wealthy estates.

So, why was the owner selling? We got our answer when we shook hands with a seventy-year-old woman, sitting in one of the salon's chairs, smelling of booze, wearing slippers and curlers in her hair.

We sat down in the office at the back of the shop, the owner pulled out a bottle of gin and filling a glass said, 'I am being robbed blind by my staff. I have lost control of the business, the final straw came yesterday when one of the girl's cousins, a guy called Alf came in a demanded one hundred dollars in protection money.'

We all sat down in the lawyer's office and signed the purchase papers; the salon owner grabbed the cheque and went. Our lawyer handed Monica some papers and a bunch of keys.

The next morning, we turned up at the new salon, Monica had brought two girls from her other salon. I had brought Two tough guys that owed me a favour, and the guy who had fixed up and decorated the last salon. Monica opened up and we all went in. The employees were four girls who worked full time at the shop and started to dwindle into the shop. Monica read the riot act, and then she fired the girl who had her cousin, Alf. She swore and walked out.

Monica introduced her two girls from the other salon, then laid down the rules about times, dress code and behaviour, as she was talking, a young tall black guy wearing baggy shorts and a skull cap walked in waving a long knife. He stood in the middle of the floor and shouted, 'Who's in charge man.' The tough guy standing next to him grabbed the knife out of his hand, and at the same, the second tough guy punched him on the cheek. He landed on the tiled floor with a bang, as he struggled to get up, both tough guys picked him up and threw him out onto the sidewalk, he lay still for a few minutes, then slowly stood up, limped to the doorway, and said, 'Can I have my knife back—please!

A week later Alice and I drove to Monica's new salon in the suburbs. It was full of clients; the staff all wore crisp white uniforms and it had been given a facelift, the decorator was finishing off the office and coffee area.

As we were speaking to one of the clients, Monica pulled up in the parking area driving a white Cadillac, she walked in with an armful of parcels, gave the parcels to the decorator, hugged me then Alice. Monica said, 'We are turning clients away, we are so busy, and I can't find any more hairdressers.

I have upped the wages of the girls in all the salons, just to hang on to them.'

Andy and his wife Sally came down from Los Angeles for the wedding. Albie and his now plump wife came the next day. Alice picked them up from Miami airport.

We all sat around the patio table drinking and eating, the guys were filling me in on the drama in Los Angeles. Andy said that they had found a cop in the special operations unit, who would tip us off on a raid, for consideration.

The wedding was to be held on the beach, there were red carpets, and flowers and everybody was dressed up, not a pair of shorts or Hawaiian shirt in sight. Alice looked beautiful as usual, walking down the red carpet with John who was going to give her away. She was crying, Monica was crying, I saw John dab his eyes. Why? I was the guy who would pay the bills, I was the one that should have been crying.

The reception was held in a plush hotel. At the speeches on the top table, the speakers were all saying what a great guy I was. Except for one person who told the truth. In my weak moment, I invited Charlie and Gina. Charlie, full of free booze insisted on making a speech. He nodded to the crowd, then, pointing to me said, 'This guy makes the mafia look like some kind of Boy Scouts' outfit, the crowd cheered, and he pointed again, this guy would sell his grandmother if the price was right,' the crowd whooped and cheered. Then Monica stood up, looked at Alice and smiled,

'I have known Alice since she was sixteen, every time she lured a guy into her bedroom, she would cut a little notch on the bedhead, by the time she was nineteen the bedhead collapsed,' Alice pulled a face, and the crowd cheered.

It was all back to the house. I had hired a couple of cooks and two waiters from Don Marchetti's restaurant. He came along as well and insisted on doing the cooking and organizing that side of the party. Gina came over and said, 'Well, well now you're a married man,' then whispered, 'But don't forget your promise of a night of passion for all the favours that I have done for you,' I nodded, and said,

'I haven't forgotten, but we will have to be a little discreet,' Gina winked,

'I am going to Zurich in the next couple of weeks, so I will give you a couple of days' notice, will that be enough?' I nodded, and Gina walked away saying, 'I can't wait, lover.' Alice and Monica came over with glasses of champagne, they were tiddly. Alice growled,

'Who was that fat bitch? One of your ex-comfort women.'

Monica handed me a glass of champagne, 'Here, this will keep your strength up, Alice said you are going to need it tonight.' they both laughed.

Charlie and Gina came over and stood next to John, who was wishing me good luck, etc, etc. Charlie was drunk and had spilt some booze down his shirt. He took a swig of booze and then said, 'We could have done a lot of business together, with my contacts and your sources of finance, we could have made a fortune.' Gina led him away back into the crowd. John carried on speaking,

'Who the hell was that guy,' I smiled, 'Just an old enemy.'

A familiar face walked towards me, it was Charlie's downtrodden wife, she shook my hand, 'Congratulations, your wife is gorgeous.' She had the usual sad face when she asked, 'Was that Charlie's girlfriend?' I smiled, 'No, I can tell you that she wouldn't touch your husband with a barge pole, she is an employee and only sticking the job for the money that he pays her to make trips abroad for his clients.'

She smiled at last. We clicked glasses then she walked off, still smiling. John returned, he was dying to tell me something, he said, 'I have found a garage that is coming up for sale next week, they have money problems, so we may get it for a knockdown price,'

I said, 'But John, it was you that told me, what if something happens to the supply from Mexico?' He smiled and said,

'Problem solved. I have started to advertise. We can buy second-hand cars, we pay off the hire purchase from the bank at a discount, and the owners are usually in arrears with the bank, so, we can buy them for a song. If we can buy the garage that is coming up for sale, that will be the perfect place for the new business,' I nodded,

'Give me time to think about that.'

That evening when all the guests had gone, I went upstairs to the bedroom, Alice was sitting on the side of the bed, naked, with a white satin nightie laid out on the bed beside her. I sat next to her, 'Why haven't you got that lovely nightie on?'

I didn't want it ripped off, I looked at her beautiful face,

'But Alice I won't rip it off,' she smiled, 'I know, but I might.'

CHAPTER 15

Pedro, my Mexican hash supplier spoke with me on the phone,

'Big trouble down here amigo, there has been a change of government, and they have let the American special forces into the job of chasing the drug producers, the Americans are finding the drug barons' jungle production bases and blowing them up or burning them to the ground. The price of all drugs has skyrocketed. I have to put my prices up, it's harder to get the hash over the border since the Americans took over. Before it was a case of a small bribe, and your stuff went across, now the Americans take the bribe and still keep the goods.' I smiled when Pedro said that there were no honest people anymore! Andy rang me and said that the police raids were increasing in Los Angeles and that the bent cop was asking for a bigger bribe to tell us when they planned to raid our hash storage houses, he also told me that he had opened a second legal advice office in downtown Los Angeles. I thought it was a crazy world!

Gina rang me, 'I am going to Zurich tomorrow, I will be on the twelve-o clock flight, see you soon?'

At the Airport lounge, Gina was sitting at the bar, looking lovely, with her red hair tied up in a bun, and those big brown eyes. She had put a whisky and ice on the top next to her chair.

'Gina, you remembered,'

'How could I forget,' she leaned over and kissed my cheek. We drank whisky and chatted till it was time to board the flight to Zurich. Gina was carrying a leather attaché case, I nodded towards the case, and said, 'The usual.' She smiled, 'Yes, a million dollars.' We booked a room at the Airport hotel and went upstairs. I stepped into the huge shower cubicle and started to wash my hair, the cubicle door opened, and Gina stepped in to join me, I have always enjoyed my back being scrubbed—and other parts of my anatomy.

After twenty minutes in the shower, I was left in a state of collapse, Gina was like a starved tiger...but who's complaining?

Gina asked me to join her at the meeting she had with the mafia types.

We sat at a huge table, Gina, and I, with four dark-suited guys with dark sunglasses who spoke to Gina in French. Gina replied in French, then handed over the attaché case. One of the guys opened the case and nodded to the others. He closed the case and then shook hands. A side door opened, and two maids walked in bearing large trays with glasses and a bottle of Bollinger La Grande champagne.

Most of the men at the table chatted to Gina in French whilst we all drank that lovely Champagne. I said to Gina, 'I didn't know you spoke fluent French,' she smiled, 'There are a lot of things that you don't know about me, and tonight I'll let you into a few more of my secrets.'

The flight back to Miami was interesting with Gina telling me about some of the characters who were American hoodlums that had done deals with the FBI, in return for a non-prison sentence, but with deportation. She said that they still did criminal activities from Zurich, but as long as they did not return to the States, they were safe from doing jail time. Gina told me, that on her first trip to meet these guys in Zurich, they had asked her if she had ever thought of ripping them off and keeping the money, they then showed her a video of a woman being stabbed and cut up into pieces with a chain saw. One guy said, that she stole less than half of what you deliver.

'We can find you anywhere you hide.' Gina said,

'I never found out what happened to my predecessor, and I didn't feel brave enough to ask, so I just did as I was told and took the money.' We flew back home. My promise was done.

At Miami Airport, I took Gina to the bar for a quick drink before we said goodbye. She had been gone ten minutes when there was a tap on my shoulder, I turned round to look at the beautiful face of Alice, she put her arms round my neck and kissed me.

On the way back to the house, she said that Monica was complaining that she never saw John as he was working all hours,

doing the rounds of the showrooms, and then when he got home, he had to return the calls and do some paperwork. Monica told her that he just fell into bed and fell asleep.

In the morning he is back on the road before dawn. Alice laughed when Monica told her that there hadn't been any fireworks in the bedroom for weeks. She shook her head and said, 'And we both know what a horny bitch she is.'

'Why don't we invite them over for the weekend and you can talk to John about Monica's moans,' I nodded. 'OK, invite them over.'

Saturday was a scorching hot day; Pedro was in the garden, wearing a huge Mexican sombrero, and the maid was preparing a salad lunch. I sat under the patio parasol with a whisky and ice, watching Alice swimming, naked as usual in the cool water of the pool. John and Monica walked through the lounge doors and came over to the patio table. John said, 'Hi man.' and sat down. Monica saw Alice and waved, then started to strip off her dress and underwear, then dived naked into the pool to join Alice, they started to giggle and chat away. I said to John, 'You will have to delegate some of the work, or you will burn out, then you will be no good to anyone if you are laid up in bed.' John nodded and said,

'You know what happens when you take your foot on the pedal.'

We arranged for a couple of the managers to take over some of the running of the garages to give John and Monica a break and take a trip to Europe. Alice still spent her Saturdays at the showroom on the coast freeway, dishing out coffee to potential buyers, flirting with some of the sales guys and generally helping out, she loved the Saturday job and had been shown the art of selling cars by some of her admirers. We would dress up and have dinner at one of Don Marchetti's pasta restaurants. He would never let us pay for anything, then we would go home, and Alice would swim in the pool, while I watched tennis on the TV in the lounge with a large whisky and ice. Life could not be any better!

John and Alice came back from their trip to Europe, all relaxed and full of stories of the sights that they had seen, John said it had done him so good to get away from the hustle and bustle of the garage business.

We sat down to lunch by the pool, Alice was chatting to Monica, who winked at her and gave the thumbs up, and then they both started laughing.

Gina rang and asked me to meet her at a downtown bar. Gina was sitting in an alcove with a glass of champagne. I got a drink from the bar and sat down in the alcove with her. She kissed my cheek and said, 'I have a proposition for you.' I took a sip and said,

'OK, I am listening.

Gina told me that one of the guys in Zurich that she delivered money to, had died in mysterious circumstances. He committed suicide by shooting himself four times in the back. We both laughed. She took a sip of the drink and then said, 'I know the code for his safe, he gave me the code when he went to Italy to do a deal. last time I saw inside that safe there were over four million American dollars, and some bearer bonds, but we would have to get into his villa, but I haven't got a key.' She said that the last time she went to the villa, a maid had let her in, but now that he is dead, the police may have sealed the doors until they solve his murder.'

She took another drink, then looked at me, 'We can split the money if we can get to it,' Gina smiled, 'It would give me independence, but I would need your help, what do you think?'

I nodded. 'It sounds like a good risk if we can get into the villa.

OK, I am up for it.'

I told Alice and John that I was going away for a few days on business, I had done this before so there were no questions to answer.

Gina was waiting at the Airport with the tickets. We had a drink in the Airport lounge and Gina explained the scenario. Gina seemed nervous on the flight to Zurich, she put her hand on my arm,

'You know what will happen if his business partners find out.' She drew her finger across her throat.

'Don't worry Gina, it will all go to plan.'

But really, I was feeling a little nervous myself.

We booked into a lakeside hotel. Then went to a restaurant to eat. Then found a taxi driver who was willing to take us ten miles out of town. It was almost dark as we got out of the taxi, and then walked up the driveway to the villa. No lights were showing from the inside of the building, we walked round to the back of the villa and found a door unlocked. Gina had a small torch, and we went upstairs, she showed me the door of the office that had the safe, it was locked. I put my shoulder to the door, and after a couple more bangs, it gave way with little trouble. Gina went straight to the safe and shone her torch onto the combination lock.

'Here, hold the torch steady.'

Gina turned the combination lock back and forth, then pulled the handle, but nothing happened. Gina swore then said,

'He has changed the combination.'

We both sat down on the floor. Gina looked at me and said,

'Sorry, I have wasted your time,' she started to sob. I said,

'Don't worry about it,' I put my arm around her shoulders. 'How old was the dead guy anyway?' Gina stiffened, smiled and said, 'That's it, I know what the new numbers are. It is his date of birth. The last code was his dead wife's date of birth.' I held the torch with a shaking hand as Gina turned the combination lock.

She tugged the handle of the safe, hey presto! It slowly opened. Revealing stacks of American dollars, piled from the bottom to the top. I found pillowcases in a cupboard and started to empty the safe, it took two pillowcases to empty the safe. Gina closed the safe and turned the combination to lock it. As we made our way downstairs, a car drove up the driveway, we quickly hid in a cleaner's cupboard, three men came into the hallway, and spoke in French for a moment, then went upstairs. Gina whispered, 'One of them said that he knew which room the safe was in.' We waited until it was all quiet, then crept out the front door, carrying the pillowcases. It was dark as we walked away from the Villa. I looked into the car sitting in the driveway. I shone the torch and saw that the keys were left on the dashboard. We jumped into the car and threw the pillowcases in the back seat.

I reversed the car out of the drive and into the road, then sped away from the villa. We drove to the edge of the town, parked up a side street, and caught a taxi back to our hotel.

In our hotel room, we emptied the pillowcases onto the bed and spent over an hour counting the money, Gina was laughing and crying, both at the same time. Gina said that there were at least six million dollars and four million in bearer bonds. Gina said,

'Well, that's five million each,' shaking my head, and said,

'I'll just have the bearer bonds. The rest is all yours. The next morning, we skipped breakfast and took a taxi into the shopping area, two large, wheeled suitcases later, we were back in the hotel filling them with dollar bills.

At the Airport, we handed in the suitcases to be delivered freight to Miami and paid the excess. In the Airport restaurant, we sat down for a meal and shared a bottle of champagne. We had two hours till our flight left.

Gina left the table and went to buy tights at the kiosk in the concourse. She came back to the table and grabbed my arm, 'Quickly stand up,' she dragged me away from the table and headed out of the restaurant. Gina said, 'I have just seen two of the gangsters who were minders for the dead guy, they know my face from previous visits to deliver money, and they will suspect that I have the code for the safe, if they see me here in Zurich, they will put two and two together if they find that the money is gone.'

We took a taxi to a back street bar and spent time there until the flight was ready to go. Then a taxi straight to the Airport and we went to departures, none of us spoke. As the plane lifted off, we hugged each other and then ordered a bottle of champagne.

At Miami airport we collected the suitcases, Gina took two suitcases and drove off with a wave. Alice picked me up in her red Ferrari like a film star. At the house, John and Monica were sitting by the pool. I put the suitcase under the patio table and jumped into the pool with all my clothes on, I was physically and mentally exhausted. John and the girls dragged me out of the pool and laughed.

They stripped me down to my underpants. Lying there, I started to sing, Dean Martins, 'Little Old Wine-drinking Me' Then the others started to sing with me, and we all broke into fits of laughter.

I left Alice to entertain the other two, then donning a dressing gown, I dragged the suitcase upstairs, then emptying it onto the bed, I counted four, one-million-dollar bearer bonds.

I had a bad feeling about this little enterprise, although the gangsters couldn't enter the States and risk jail, they had contacts and money, when they found that the money in the villa was missing, they would soon work out the people who had access, and having to kill a few people until they killed the right one would not bother them, to them it wasn't all about the money, it was also about respect. An insult could get you killed!

The trouble started when I got a call from Charlie, he said that Gina had told him that she quit the job, then she sold her apartment and bought a seven-bedroom house with a pool in an upmarket suburb of Miami, with a Cadillac convertible on the driveway. Charlie said, 'Where the hell did she get the money from?'

I shook my head and thought—we are in deep trouble.

Alice had her twenty-second birthday party at the house, she invited everyone she knew, and she knew a lot of people.

Don Marchetti organized the food and Monica ordered the booze, with some of the car sales guys working as waiters.

Gina was with a tall pretty boy kind of a guy. She brought him over and said, 'This is Donnie, then she said, Donnie go fetch us a drink,' when he had gone Gina whispered, 'We did it, we did it, and smiled.' I lowered my voice and said, 'Gina cool it, these guys from Zurich are still trying to find out who stole the money. They aren't going to stir up trouble here in Miami in case the FEDS start to take notice of them, But I won't be visiting Zurich anytime soon!

Charlie came over with his wife, 'Nice party that Alice has thrown, do you know that people are asking about Gina and where her money came from? I got a call from a guy who said, were you in on the heist in Zurich? Charlie's mobile rang, he put it to his ear and after five seconds he handed me the phone, and said, 'Someone wanted to talk to you. I put the phone to my ear, there was a moment of silence, and then Gina spoke in a croaky voice,

'They beat me, I had to tell them everything!'

The phone was answered by the stranger, 'Give the money back, or Gina dies.' then the phone went dead.

Opening my safe I took out my revolver, stuck it in my trouser belt, then took the tiny derringer and put it down my sock, I drove Moe's black Cadillac over to Gina's house. It was an hour's drive to her house. And when I pulled up outside her door, the door was half open, walking into the huge lobby, Gina was sitting in a chair, bound with tape and with a bullet hole in her head.

Those beautiful eyes were wide open, I put my hand over her face and closed her eyes.

The gun was pressed against my head and a hand pulled my gun from the trouser belt, turning round, I faced two guys, one was a little scruffy dude with a half-smoked cigar sticking out the side of his mouth, and the other guy had a pocked marked face and was holding a huge six-shooter, and with a Cowboy hat on the back of his head, 'Where is the money.' The little guy asked. Nodding, I said, 'Why did you have to kill her,' the cowboy looked at his friend,

'I guess that was you,' they both laughed, 'Sorry, but a contract was put out on both of you guys, but if you give us the money, we will let you go, they looked at each other and grinned.

'OK, guys, you can have the money, it's in a safe at my house, there are five million in cash.' Their eyes lit up. The cowboy said,

'Just give us the combination and we will let you live' The little guy said 'Yes, only the combination and you can walk away. We will tell the guys who gave us the contract that we killed you.' They were getting excited at the thought of getting five million dollars.

'Look guys you will need more than the combination to get the money, there is a catch that you have to press in a certain way to open the safe once you have done the combination, if you press the catch the wrong way the safe automatically locks up,

so I will have to go with you and show you how to open the safe.'

The Cowboy pointed his gun at my head, and growled, 'If this is a trick, we will kill everyone we find in your house.'

We went outside, the guys had parked their car around the back of Gina's house. I had to sit in the front with the cowboy who drove, the little guy sat in the back with a gun pointed at my head. We got out at my house, Alice was sitting in a patio chair, reading a magazine, she dropped the magazine and stood up when she saw the guys had guns.

The little guy smiled, 'Nice setup you have here,' The Cowboy said to Alice, 'Go make some coffee, bitch.' We all sat at the table drinking coffee when suddenly, the little guy grabbed Alice by the wrist and said, 'Hey, look at the size of the rock,' He put his gun in his pocket and pulled the ring off her finger, Alice struggled with him, shouting 'You piece of shit, this is mine.' The little guy pulled his gun out of his pocket, I said, 'Alice, give him the ring, you are worth more than some ring to me,' she paused and handed her ring to him. The little guy looked at the ring and then put it on his little finger. The Cowboy said, 'Now let's get the money, and get out of here. The Cowboy told the little guy, 'Stay with her if this guy tries any funny business and doesn't come up with the money, shoot her.' The Cowboy stuck his revolver in my back as we walked up the stairs. I opened the door that covered the safe and then started to turn the combination. I stopped and reached into my trouser pocket; the Cowboy put his gun to my head. 'What are you doing? 'I said,

'I can't remember the long number, but it's on a slip of paper that I keep in my pocket,' I handed him a folded piece of paper with a phone number written in pencil, and he read it out to me.

He had to use both hands to open the note, as he put his gun in the air to use his hand. I pulled out my derringer and stuck it into his neck. I had practised this move till I could like a magic trick.

He froze, I grabbed his gun smacked him on the side of his head, and whispered, 'Call the little guy up here, tell him that you need him to help carry the money.' I cocked the six-shooter and stood behind him. He shouted down,

'Jake, kill the girl if I am not down there in two minutes.' He turned Turning round to face me, 'Now what?'

I pushed him down the stairs in front of me. On the patio, the little guy was standing behind Alice with a gun pointing at her head. Alice was shaking with fear. It was a Mexican stand-off. I said,

'Let's do a deal guys, I'll give you a million each and you can walk away, just let the girl go, and put down your gun, the little guy said, 'You put your gun down or I will shoot the bitch.'

The Cowboy grinned, 'It looked like you have an awkward situation' I shouted, 'Alice, remember the ass bump game?' The little guy said, 'Let my friend go now, or she is a goner, just like your red-headed friend in the big house.' The little guy was behind Alice, she moved back a little, and the little guy said,

'Stand still bitch.' Alice suddenly bumped the little guy hard with her butt. He staggered backwards falling into the pool, dropping his gun into the water. I pushed the Cowboy to the edge of the pool, Alice dived into the pool. I shouted, 'What the hell are you doing Alice,' she shouted back, 'This piece of shit has my ring.' The little guy was struggling shouting and splashing, he could not swim, Alice was struggling to take her ring off the little guy's finger, he didn't struggle with her and she got her ring back, then. Then slapped his face, and spat out, 'That's for taking my ring.'

With Alice holding a gun, I taped them up to the patio chairs. 'Who sent you,' Cowboy said, 'All we got told was if we bumped off two guys, we would get paid fifty thousand dollars each, we never met the contract, but they gave us the name of a local contact who would give us the addresses of the targets?'

'Who was that.' the little guy said, 'Some dude called Charlie?' I could not believe my ears,

'Describe him,' The little guy said,

'A short fat, bald dude.' I put the two guys into their car, and with Alice driving we went back to Gina's house to pick up my Cadillac

We parked in the front driveway, then dragged the patio chairs with the guys still taped up, into the lobby.

Putting the Cowboy's six shooter on the floor beside Gina, outside.

Outside I rang the cops and gave them the address, piled into the Cadillac and drove home.

As we climbed into bed, Alice kissed me good night and spoke.

'That was a nice touch, you saying that I was worth more than any stupid ring,' I didn't tell her that I had it insured for a small fortune.

Did Charlie, really tell those killers where Gina lived, knowing that when they found her, they were going to kill her? Even for Charlie, this was terrible, I was going to make him pay for this, he was a guy with no loyalty or morals. He knew that when he gave them her address, she was as good as dead. One of the people who owed me a favour was the assistant state prosecutor, Ann, I had saved her from being blackmailed by Charlie, the struck-off lawyer. It could have cost her the position of state prosecutor. and her marriage. She told me that if there was anything that she could legally help me with, she would. We met in her office. She stood up and shook my hand, then left the office, ten minutes later she returned with a tray of coffee. Smiling, Ann said, 'How can I help.' Over coffee, I explained that her old blackmailer had caused me great pain and that he had a hand in the murder of a dear friend. Ann sipped her coffee, and thought for a moment, then said,

'The only way that I can help you is if Charlie did something illegal, like act for a client in a legal situation or be involved in a shady deal, but you would have to have the evidence. Although Charlie is struck off from practising law in the state of Florida, he is still a savvy guy who knows the Law.'

Alice came with me to the golf club; I had a meeting with Charlie. We sat at a table with drinks, then he told me that he had to take the cash from his Clients in Miami to Zurich himself until he found someone that he could trust. He asked Alice would you like the job? She shook her head. Over a drink, he showed us a brown leather attaché case, and he winked,

'Tomorrow I fly to Zurich with a million dollars in this baby,' he patted the case. Charlie went to the bar with Alice for drinks.

While they were at the bar, I took a good look at the name of the case. I told Charlie that I would see if I could find someone to take the money to Zurich, somebody he could trust.

On the way back to town, I said to Alice, 'Now we have to find a shop that sells that same make of attaché case if my plan is to work.' We parked outside an expensive leather store, inside, we looked around, but we didn't see the make or colour of the case. Two young assistants came over, and asked, 'Can we help,? Alice shook her head, 'We are looking for a particular make and colour of case,'

the small sales guy said, 'I have never heard of that brand, it may be a discontinued line. Fashions change, last year it was leather, this year it's plastic, next year...?'

We turned to walk away when the other taller sales guy, said, 'Wait, I remember one of our customers searching for that make of case, he told us later that he had found the make of case that you just asked for.' The sales guy could not remember the store but said, 'I may have his name on file.' He went over to the computer sitting on the sales counter and started tapping into the keyboard. A big smile came over his face,

'I found his telephone number.' He picked up the phone on his desk and rang, as he spoke, he wrote on a slip of paper. Putting the phone down, he handed me the slip of paper with the name of the store.

Alice handed them twenty bucks each, nodding,

'Thanks, guys.' Driving over to the store, Alice said 'What if the store is out of stock?' I shook my head, 'I'll just have to think of another way to trap that dude.' Inside the store a little girl with pigtails came from the back room, we explained what brand we were looking for. She shook her head straight away, 'Sorry, we don't stock that brand anymore.' As we went to the door, an old guy with coffee stains down his shirt, and dark glasses perched on the end of his nose, walked through from the stockroom. Holding a cup of coffee. He said,' I heard your enquiry.' Then said to the pigtailed girl,

'Have a look in returns, I am sure we have one there,

but it might not be the colour you are looking for.' Alice held her hands up with her fingers crossed. The girl walked back through the shop smiling and holding the exact model and colour. The old guy inspected the case. 'I am afraid it was returned because it has a stiff lock, but I can give you a discount if you want to take the case.' Alice handed the old guy a hundred-dollar bill, and we left.

I rang the cop that I had saved from being blackmailed and asked him where I could get ten thousand dollars-worth of cocaine.

We met at a downtown hotel, the cop was wearing jeans and a tee shirt, with a baseball cap. Two huge black guys, carrying a shopping bag, walked into the hotel and joined us. The cop spoke with them, then handed me the shopping bag, I handed the cop a large envelope with the ten thousand dollars.

We all shook hands and left. At the house, Alice helped me fill the leather case with the cocaine, then locked the case. The last part of the plan was to get down to the Airport before Charlie left for Switzerland.

Charlie tapped me on the shoulder, 'What are you doing here?' He sat on the next stool, and put his case down, next to his leg. We were having a drink and chatting when two guys came to the bar and ordered drinks. Another guy came up to the bar and stood on the other side of me. He leaned over, with a cigar in his hand, 'Do you have a light?' Charlie took out his lighter and leaning over me, lit the guy's cigar, the guy nodded, 'Thanks man,' then took his drink and left the bar. The other two guys also went. Charlie finished his drink, shook my hand and waved goodbye. Picking up his case, he walked over to departures. As I watched Charlie's flight take off, I was joined by the three guys who were at the bar, one of them handed me a leather attaché case, and the guy with the cigar shook my hand. I handed each one a thousand bucks, 'Thanks, guys.' Outside the Airport a big black car had the window wound down.

Sitting inside was Ann. The state prosecutor smiled, 'All done?' I nodded. Ann said, 'My department is in touch with the Swiss customs at Zurich Airport.' The window went up and the car drove off.

Back at the house, I opened the leather attaché case onto the patio table, one million dollars was neatly stacked inside.

At Zurich Airport, Charlie was walking to the taxi rank at the Airport exit. When three police officers and two customs men, surrounded him, one customs man took the case and said,

'Please follow us, sir."

Charlie was feeling confident, inside the customs office, the case was put on the table and Charlie looked at the customs man holding the case, he grinned, 'You are making a mistake, I have an agreement with a bank to carry large sums of American dollars into Zurich.'

'Will you open the case, sir, the lock appears to be sticking.' Charlie wrenched the case open; a cloud of white dust rose. Charlie looked at the Cocaine in horror. He struggled as the cops put the handcuffs on his wrists. One of the customs men said,

'And have you an agreement with a drug supplier to carry Cocaine into Zurich?' Everyone smiled, except Charlie.

At his trial in the Supreme Court in Zurich. Charlie was sentenced to Twelve years of jail time. As for the million dollars that he should have delivered. He was told that the mafia boss who should have received the money, had put a contract on him in prison. Almost six months later, Charlie was found in the prison showers, stabbed to death. By then, his wispy grey hair had turned white.

CHAPTER 16

Alice and I stood at Gina's gravestone, I laid a bunch of her favourite red roses onto the grass, then kissed the headstone,
 'Sleep well my love, sleep well.
I got a call to come to a lawyer's office. His secretary showed me to a chair. The lawyer put on his glasses and read a document to me. '
Gina left her entire estate to me. Her house and two million dollars.

John and Monica would often come over for dinner. The girls would chatter about what was happening at the salons or the car showrooms. While John would fill me in on what was happening in the car business. Leaving the car business all to him, I had kept a hold of the bulk buying process. I and my contact would have a round of golf and sort out the price of the next car delivery, then I would slip him a five hundred dollar note over a drink in the clubhouse.
 All was well. The hash money from Los Angeles was continuing to flow in every month, even with the price hike. The safe in the house was full, so I had another bigger safe installed in the garage. Apart from the millions in the bank and the safe, I had twelve million in bearer bonds. A half share in eight car showrooms and garages and the deeds to seven buildings where Monica had her salons. Charlie's wife received an insurance payout from Charlie's murder in prison. The next time that I bumped into her she was completely changed. Her hair was permed and dyed hazel, a little makeup with new glasses and smart clothes. Looking ten years younger, she seemed a lot happier.
 I had over eighteen million dollars stashed away in banks, bearer bonds and investments. A half share in a chain of car sales sites and garages, Sitting by our patio table having drinks with John and Monica,
 Alice stood up, looked at me and smiled.
 'I have a little surprise for you,' she patted her belly with both hands. Monica stood up next to her, looked over to John, smiled and patted her belly and said, 'Ditto.'

George and Alice had a son, Hank Junior, named after Alice's father. Followed one year later by Audrey, their daughter.

Two years later, on a visit to Los Angeles, George was shot dead by Mexican drug dealers.

As per his instructions, his body was taken back to Scotland and buried in a small Brethren graveyard, overlooking the sea.

Rufusdog@live.co.uk

From the Author

Your voice truly matters, so if you enjoyed this novel, it would mean the world if you took a short minute to leave a heartfelt review on Amazon. Your kind feedback is very appreciated and so very important. Thank you so much for your time.

Printed by Amazon Italia Logistica S.r.l.
Torrazza Piemonte (TO), Italy

56385246R00075